JUST FOR

NOW

SHERRYL D. HANCOCK

Published by Vulpine Press in the United Kingdom in 2019

ISBN 978-1-83919-282-1

Cover by Claire Wood

www.vulpine-press.com

Also in the *MidKnight Blue* series:

CHAPTER 1

Things were decidedly tense in the chief's office. With Julio Martinez, the man who'd already tried to kill Midnight Chevalier once, on the loose from Mexican police custody, the entire department was on edge, wondering where he'd turned up.

Stevie O'Neil could sense the palpable tension as she walked into Midnight's outer office for her appointment with the chief. Cassandra, Midnight's secretary, glanced up and motioned her into Midnight's office; the door was already open.

Stevie knocked on the door jamb. Midnight was standing at her desk, phone in hand. Rick Debenshire was there as well as Joe Sinclair. There was another man standing in the office too. Midnight glanced up and motioned for Stevie to come in and have a seat.

"Yes," Midnight said into the phone, "I understand. Thank you." She hung up.

"What did he say?" Rick asked.

"He said there's only so much he can do with the limited security they have at the school."

Rick looked at Joe. "You got patrol alerted, then?"

"Yeah, I'm on it," Joe said. "I'll have them head over now."

"Good," Rick said, his tone serious.

Midnight glanced over at Stevie. "Sorry, things are a bit stressed right now."

"It's okay," Stevie said. "Do you want me to come back later?"

"No, I'm almost ready. Can you hang out a few?"

"Of course." Stevie was surprised that the chief was asking. Like she had anything else to do.

Dave walked in, glancing at Stevie then looking directly at Midnight. Midnight waited expectantly.

"I got no leads, boss," Dave said unhappily. "He's got no connections here as far as I can tell."

Midnight pursed her lips, looking over at Rick, who looked increasingly tense. "We'll find him," she told her husband.

"We'd better," Rick said, his arms crossed in front of him.

Midnight walked over to him, looking up into his eyes. "We'll find him, babe."

Rick's face softened. He reached out and touched her cheek. "I can't lose you again," he said softly.

"You won't," Midnight assured him. "Go on, I need to handle this." She gestured with her head to Stevie. "Joe, let me know if you get any hits."

"Will do," Joe said, turning and leaving with Rick. Dave walked out, giving Stevie a long, measured look then a quick wink, closing the door behind him.

The man Stevie didn't know sat down in the chair next to her, and Midnight took her seat as well.

"Stevie, this is Kyle Masterson—he just started as the Assistant Chief here. Kyle, this is Stevie O'Neil."

Stevie turned to Kyle. She extended her hand to him. "Good to meet you, sir."

"You too, Ms. O'Neil," Kyle responded warmly.

Midnight sat back in her chair, giving Stevie a considering look. "First of all, Stevie, we need to establish a couple of things."

"Yes, ma'am," Stevie replied automatically, steeling herself for what was to come, still not convinced she wasn't about to be arrested.

"Were you responsible for the body of Ramon Calderon?" Midnight asked, referring to the man who had been killed in his apartment.

Stevie's face was like stone as she calmly replied, "Yes."

"What happened?" Kyle asked authoritatively.

"Tiempo sent me to his apartment with a message about a shipment. Calderon decided that I was the message and was up for grabs." Stevie's voice was still calm, but her green eyes sparkled with remembered anger. "He made his play—I told him no."

"What happened then?" Midnight asked, leaning forward, her hands on the desk in front of her.

Stevie moved her neck as if working out a kink, her eyes closing for a second. Then she opened them, looking directly into Midnight's eyes. "He pulled out a large hunting knife with a six-inch serrated blade and told me we could do it the easy way or the hard way. I pulled my weapon and told him that he could put the knife down or he could die. He didn't believe me and took a step toward me."

"How far away from you was he then?" Kyle put in, his eyes narrowing slightly.

"About eight feet."

Kyle nodded. "Please, go on."

Stevie nodded too. "I fired one shot, hitting him in the right thigh. He didn't stop. He took another step—I told him to stop. It was obvious to me that he was on something, probably meth—that was his drug of choice. When he took the next step, I fired again. He wouldn't stop. When he was approximately three feet from me, I fired the final shot to the head."

"You had reasonable fear for your life," Kyle said, looking over at Midnight and nodding. Stevie's story jibed exactly with everything the forensic analysts had come back with, even the fact that the final shot had been fired from approximately three feet. Calderon had indeed had a large quantity of methamphetamine in his bloodstream.

Midnight leaned forward, her expression intense, her eyes on Stevie. "I want you to know here and now that what you did, going after Tiempo on your own, although very brave and for seemingly good reasons, is *not* how we do things in this department. Is that understood?" Midnight's voice left no room for argument. It was obvious she was very serious and that there was an underlying threat in her statement.

"Yes, ma'am," Stevie replied. She knew Midnight could easily have arrested her for the killing of Calderon, at least for the purposes of investigation. She was willing to agree that what she had done was outside the realm of law enforcement.

Midnight gave her a searching look, looking for signs of deception. She saw none in the other woman's eyes. She sat back in her chair again.

"Now that we have that established," she said, her lips twisting in a half grin, "what do I do with you?"

"Ma'am?" Stevie queried, not sure what Midnight meant and half afraid she was talking in terms of being charged. Had she just walked into a trap, admitting to killing Calderon? But that didn't conform with what she thought she knew about Midnight's style.

Midnight shook her head, seeing the sudden apprehension on Stevie's face. "Relax, O'Neil. Do you still have that badge I tossed you the other day?"

"Yes, ma'am," Stevie said, producing it from her pocket and moving to hand it to Midnight.

Midnight held up her hand. "Keep it, and"—she opened her desk drawer and pulled out a small flat box and an envelope—"take these too." She pushed them across the desk.

Stevie leaned forward, taking the items slowly. She opened the box and stared almost in awe at the duty weapon and ammunition clip nestled in foam. Her finger traced the barrel of the weapon as she shook her head. Then she set the weapon in its box on the desk and opened the envelope. In it were credentials that identified her as a peace officer and the requisition form for her duty equipment. She hadn't truly believed until that moment that she would really get her job back. She had figured Dave was just hoping for her benefit that she would.

"Ma'am…" she breathed, not sure what to say right then. "I don't know how to thank you, to tell you, to explain what this means…" Her voice trailed off as she felt a lump rise in her throat.

"You just did," Midnight said as she smiled understandingly.

Stevie bit the inside of her lip, feeling very overwhelmed.

"As for assignments," Midnight began, "I can't exactly put you back out on the street right now—you're too hot."

Stevie nodded, chagrined that she was basically a target for any of the people Tiempo had had dealings with and, therefore, once again a liability to the department.

"So I think I've come up with the best solution," Midnight continued, placing her hands on a folder in front of her, turning it around and pushing it toward Stevie. "I've created a training and development position for you as a sergeant. If you agree to it, you'll receive the mid-range salary as a patrol officer but you will be training as a sergeant. When the test comes up, you'll take it, and if you score in the top three ranks, I'll promote you, and you'll begin making sergeant's pay at that time. We're looking at about six months until the next test comes up. Are you interested?"

Stevie stared blankly at Midnight for a few long moments, stunned. Sergeant? Officers waited years to take that test! She wouldn't have dreamed of making sergeant for at least six years. She knew she was being handed a golden opportunity here, and she knew she should grab it and run, but she had to know why.

"Sergeant..." Stevie said, as if testing the title, then looked at Midnight, her eyes narrowing slightly in her morbid curiosity. "But why?"

Midnight grinned, realizing that Stevie's sense of propriety was warring with her desire to grab the brass ring. She shrugged. "Basically, you've made yourself too hot to put out on the street in a uniform, and, as far as I'm concerned, you've proven your ability to do investigative and infiltration work. My best narc couldn't take Tiempo down alone—you facilitated that. Besides, I think ingenuity and uncommon valor deserve recognition—don't you?"

Again Stevie was left speechless. To have someone like Midnight

Chevalier, who was basically a legend in the law enforcement community, telling her she was brave was just astounding.

"Do you want the job, O'Neil?" Midnight asked, her look indicating that she would think Stevie was nuts if she said no.

"Yes, ma'am," Stevie replied, her voice stronger this time.

"Good," Midnight said, looking over at Kyle and rolling her eyes. "Thought I was going to have to sell it somewhere else for a minute there." Midnight's grin started, and Kyle chuckled, which made Stevie relax immediately.

"Ms. O'Neil," Kyle said warmly. "Do you happen to know anything about cyberspace?"

"In terms of what?" Stevie asked, her brows furrowing in confusion.

"In terms of chat rooms and that type of thing."

"I've chatted a few times," Stevie said, still confused. "But nothing major—not my thing. Why?"

"Well," Kyle began, shifting in his chair to turn toward her as he spoke, "we'd like you to work with one of the people under me on a special project. A kind of a pilot project."

"Okay," Stevie said, nodding.

"The man you need to see is Christian Collins. He's our computer expert—you'll be working with him. He can give you all the details and get you set up."

"Yes, sir," she replied, still feeling a bit dumbfounded by all of this.

Midnight stood up, signaling an end to the meeting. Stevie and Kyle stood as well.

"Stevie," Midnight said, extending her hand to the other woman. "It's good to have you back."

"Thank you, ma'am," Stevie said, clasping Midnight's hand. "I won't let you down."

"I know you won't." Midnight nodded toward the folder still sitting on the desk in front of Stevie. "Read that paperwork over and sign it, and we'll get you back on board officially."

"I'll do that," Stevie said, turning to Kyle and extending her hand. "It was nice meeting you, sir. I'll contact Mr. Collins this morning, if I can locate him."

"He's in the same office as your sister," Midnight put in, smiling.

Stevie laughed. "That should make it relatively easy, then."

Once outside Midnight's office, Stevie breathed a sigh of relief. She couldn't believe her luck. Not only had she gotten her job back, but basically she'd just gotten a promotion. She could almost hear Jason saying "spoiled brat," as he'd often called her when he was alive. She grinned to herself as she walked down the hallway toward the elevators. A few minutes later she was walking into her sister's office.

Rhiannon wasn't at her desk, but she heard someone tapping away at the keys of a computer. She stuck her head around the high cubicle walls and encountered the back of a monitor.

"Hello?" she said.

"Yeah?" replied a disembodied voice.

"Uh," Stevie stammered, feeling odd talking to the back of a monitor. "I'm looking for Christian Collins."

"And who are you?" asked the distinctly English-accented voice.

Tired of talking to the computer, Stevie moved to the side so she could see the operator of the machine. It had been many, many years since she'd been left speechless by a man's looks, but she was indeed devoid of speech when she set eyes on this man. He was dressed in a black shirt, jeans, and black suede shoes. He had jet black hair well past his collar, and was looking back at her insolently with light blue eyes fringed with long black lashes, one eyebrow quirked.

"I'm, uh…" Stevie stammered, clearing her throat to try and regain her composure quickly. "Stevie O'Neil."

"Ah," the man replied. "The renegade cop."

Stevie's eyes narrowed. She was sure now that she did know who she was talking to, and didn't like the label he'd just placed on her. "And you're Christian Collins, the cop killer."

"We should make a lovely pair, eh?" Christian replied, grinning at Stevie's annoyance.

Stevie opened her mouth to say something cutting, but then it hit her that he was baiting her. She closed her mouth, making a disgusted sound in the back of her throat. Christian's grin widened.

"Come on," he said, standing up and stretching. "Let's get some coffee." With that, he stepped around her and headed out of the office. Stevie caught up with him as he walked out the door.

They said nothing all the way down in the elevator. Christian leaned calmly against the wall, his arms crossed over his chest. An Asian man Stevie knew as Spider Nguyen got on the elevator.

"Hey, Blue," Spider said.

"Spider," Christian replied, nodding at the other man.

Spider got off when they did on the ground floor. Christian said, "Later man."

9

Spider replied with a simple "Later," but grinned. On the way into the coffee shop on the corner, they encountered Donovan Curtis and his fiancée, Jeanie Franco. Donovan and Christian shook hands, and Jeanie hugged Christian and kissed him on the cheek, saying it had been a while since she'd seen him. Stevie looked on, noting that Christian Collins was indeed a member of "the Gang."

When they got up to the counter, the server, a young woman with an eyebrow piercing, winked at Christian. "The usual, Blue?"

"Yeah," Christian said, grinning at her, then gestured to Stevie. "And whatever she's having."

Stevie ordered a mocha with a double shot of espresso.

"Heavy night?" Christian asked, his look impertinent.

"Every night is," Stevie replied brazenly.

"Oh…" Christian drawled, sounding intrigued, his light blue eyes sparkling with mischief. Stevie couldn't help but grin.

They got their orders and went to sit in a corner. Christian leaned back, his long legs extended in front of him. "Seriously," he said, his tone conciliatory, "I heard you did real well for yourself out there."

Stevie was surprised by his apparent attempt to reconcile their differences. She nodded. "And I heard you were justified in shooting the bastard."

That garnered a bark of laughter from the Englishman as he nodded. "He did shoot first."

"Fight fire with fire, my dad always said."

Again Christian laughed and nodded agreement. In that moment, they became fast friends.

At noon that day, Midnight received a frantic phone call from the principal at Mikeyla's school.

"The man said we were to send Chief Chevalier's daughter out in fifteen minutes or he'd blow up the school with a bomb he has hidden on campus!" The woman sounded half hysterical. "We've only got thirteen minutes!" she wailed.

"We'll be there in five," Midnight said, hanging up and yelling to Cassandra even as she picked the phone up again and dialed Joe's extension. Kyle was in her office, so he got on his cell phone and called Rick.

Police cars converged on La Jolla Middle School in a record three minutes. The bomb squad was there too, with eight teams of dogs and handlers searching every room. Meanwhile, officers herded frightened but controlled teenagers to the auditorium.

Julio Martinez swore viciously under his breath. Puta! How did she react so fast? They'd quickly discover that there was no bomb. Of course there wasn't; he hadn't had time to create a bomb, let alone set one. He had hoped to bluff and get the girl; then he'd bring the puta to him and kill her and her daughter, and maybe even the husband too if he was lucky. This was not his lucky day though. How did she know he wouldn't blow up the school with her brat in it?

Slamming his fist into the nearest wall, Julio let off another string of expletives. The blond bitch steals his son and has him thrown in that hole of a prison and she thinks she can get away with it? No! No one treats Julio Martinez like a dog! The bitch would pay—he'd see to that.

"How did you know he wouldn't blow up the school?" the frightened principal asked, squinting up at the tall blond Englishman.

"Because he just escaped prison late last night. There was no way he had time to set a bomb," Joe replied. The woman just nodded, and walked away wringing her hands.

Joe's cell phone rang.

"'Lo."

"Is it clear?" Rick asked, his voice tense.

"Yeah, it's clear," Joe replied, beckoning Mikeyla to him as he talked. "Keyl is fine. I'll have her at the office in about twenty minutes. You can both relax for now."

"Thanks, man."

Rick had made Midnight stay in the office, afraid that if she showed up at the school, Martinez would try to take her out again. In turn, Midnight had insisted that Rick stay too, afraid that Martinez would be all too happy to take out her spouse.

Midnight had the area scoured, but Martinez had cleared out. None of them slept well that night.

***

Jeanie Franco wasn't sleeping well either. She'd received a letter that day that she'd been waiting for, but now she wasn't sure what to do. The letter had come to her mother's house, which she'd given as her mailing address. Her mother had called that afternoon, waking her up. Jeanie had thrown on sweatpants and a T-shirt and driven over to pick it up.

The letter was from Alcoholic Beverage Control, and they were offering her a job as an investigator. It was exactly what she wanted. It was a chance to get away from the hideous job of patrol, which she hated, and her FTO, who was a total male chauvinist jerk. It was a chance to do investigation work and make cases, like she'd helped Donovan to do three years before. There was only one major catch— the job was in San Francisco.

Jeanie hadn't told Donovan she was applying. In truth, she didn't believe at first that she'd actually have a chance. One of the guys at the department who had been in her academy class had told her he was going for it. He'd said that if she was smart, she'd do the same; it was a chance to get out of patrol. Of course, that guy was lucky enough to get assigned to San Diego. The man at the field office for ABC had told her when she'd picked up the application that there were still a couple of spots left in San Diego, so she'd gone ahead and applied. By the time she'd taken the written exam, however, those spots had been filled, and she'd known she was applying for a job out of town.

A couple of months before, while Donovan was on a case, she'd gone up to San Francisco for the oral interview and physical agility. She'd told him she was visiting friends. While she'd been there, she'd picked up information on San Francisco Police Department's narcotics unit, thinking that on the off chance she got the job with ABC, Donovan could easily get on with SFPD.

Now that she'd actually been offered a job, though, she was terrified. She knew she should have told Donovan about this long before now. But in the end it had been easier just to continue the process and "see what happens." Now it had happened, and now she needed to tell Donovan. She'd spent a lot of nights awake trying to figure out how to approach it. The date she was to report to the ABC academy in Huntington Beach was fast approaching, and she couldn't wait anymore.

When Donovan came in that night he noted that Jeanie had ordered Chinese food, all his favorites. He was fairly pleased, since he'd had a long day at work and didn't feel like cooking. He'd been thinking he'd take her to dinner, since it was her night off, but this was better. They ate together at the dining room table, talking about work, and about what had happened that day with Midnight's daughter. Julio Martinez brought up a lot of terrifying memories for Jeanie as well, making her remember the night she'd heard that a San Diego police officer had been killed in Mexico, knowing that Donovan and Midnight were down there. At the time, the news hadn't announced which officer had been killed. She had had no idea if it had been Donovan. In the end, she'd made her brother take her to Mexico so she could find out.

Donovan had been thrown through a plate-glass window in the blast, but had survived it with mostly minor cuts and some injury to his back. He'd been extremely lucky. Jeanie had been extremely grateful to the powers that be. It had been then that she'd been sure that she loved him. The trip they had taken after that horrible time had been when Donovan asked her to marry him. She still loved him every bit as much as she had then. That was why she was convinced that this would work out.

After dinner they moved to the couch, drinking wine and still talking. That eventually proceeded to kissing. Not long after that, Donovan carried her to their bed and made love to her. Afterward, she knew she needed to talk to him. Every minute that passed made her feel like she was lying to him by not saying anything.

"Donovan?" she began quietly. She lay on her side, her back against his chest, his arms encircling her.

"Mmm?" he murmured sleepily, his lips against her neck.

Jeanie turned over to face him. The hall light was still on, so she could see him clearly in the dimness.

"I need to talk to you."

"Okay," he said, grinning as his hand slid over her hip to her waist, pulling her close to him again and kissing her forehead. "Talk." His voice was soft and languid; he was very relaxed.

"What do you think of San Francisco?" she asked, biting her lower lip.

Donovan blinked a couple of times, trying to assimilate the question.

"San Francisco?" he repeated.

"You know, the city," Jeanie supplied, grinning to try and keep the mood light.

"Oh yeah, the city." Donovan grinned in return, then shrugged. "Haven't thought much about it. I've only been there once."

"Did you like it?"

"It was alright. Why?" Donovan asked, still not comprehending this line of questioning, thinking she wanted to go on vacation or something.

"Would you ever consider living there?"

Donovan laughed lightly. "Why would I want to do that?"

"Well," Jeanie said, biting her lip again and looking up at him. "Because I might be going there."

"What for?" Donovan asked, his tone deepening now.

"For a job, Donovan," Jeanie said, her voice beseeching him to hear her out. "I've been offered a job with Alcoholic Beverage Control as an investigator, but it's in San Francisco."

"Offered a job?" Donovan echoed, his brows furrowing, the investigator in him coming out immediately. "How did this happen?"

"Well, I applied," Jeanie said, trying to keep it simple—but it wasn't going to be that easy.

"When?"

"I…" Jeanie began. She knew she was in the wrong right now, and that there was no way out of the truth. "I applied three months ago."

Donovan's expression changed, and she could sense his anger. "And when did you plan to tell me?"

"I didn't think I was going to get the job."

"So why not tell me?"

"I just… I don't know," Jeanie said, feeling trapped. "I just wanted to see if I'd get on, then figure out if I was going to take it."

Donovan nodded, his face a mask of disbelief, his teal eyes narrowed.

"Donovan," Jeanie went on, grasping at her one hope. "I checked out San Francisco PD's narcotics unit—they have a huge one—and I know—"

"You checked it out? When?" Donovan's eyes narrowed further, and the ice crept into his voice. "You mean when you were 'visiting friends' in San Francisco?"

16

Jeanie's eyes widened. She knew she'd just been caught in a lie. "Donovan, I just didn't—"

"You lied to me, Jeanie. Why?" His voice was so cold she could feel it, and suddenly she knew she had to convince him that San Francisco PD would work for him.

"I'm sorry, okay? I just didn't want to tell you just then. But look, SFPD is one of the biggest departments in the country. Their narcotics unit is huge—you could get on with them no problem. The guy in personnel told me they always need experienced narcs."

"I already have a job, Jeanie," Donovan said, moving to sit up.

Jeanie sat too, grabbing her shirt to pull it on. The last thing she wanted to do was fight with him while she was naked.

"I know that, Donovan, but you could have one there too."

"Now, why would I want to do that?" Donovan was looking down at her as if he didn't even know her anymore.

Jeanie stared up at him, so surprised by his attitude that she didn't know what to say.

"See, I have a job here, and a house here, and a life here, Jeanie."

"Donovan…" Jeanie began, trying a different tack. "You know I hate patrol—I can't do it anymore. I swear I'm going to shoot my FTO soon. You have to understand that!"

"Oh, I understand," Donovan said, his tone not indicating understanding at all. "I understand that you want things right now, that you don't want to put in the time to get what you want."

"That's not fair," Jeanie said, hurt.

"No, Jay, that's the thing—it is fair. You can't be an investigator without putting in the time on the street. You need that time on the street to teach you things they can't teach in the academy."

"Bullshit!" Jeanie shouted. "All I'm learning from that asshole I have for an FTO is that women don't belong in law enforcement. That we're all just being indulged because the chief is a woman. That we don't really do law enforcement, that we're all window dressing."

Donovan sat back against the headboard, staring at the ceiling. "I told you to go talk to Joe or even Midnight about the guy's attitude."

"No, Donovan, I'm not going running to Joe or Midnight every time I have a problem," Jeanie snapped.

"No, you'll just run away."

Jeanie sucked in her breath. She wasn't running away; she was doing something for herself.

"I want to be an investigator. I know I can do it. I had hoped you'd support me on this. I support you in what you do."

Donovan's eyes locked with hers as he stared back at her for a long moment. "I guess the main difference here is I never asked you to quit your job and leave your life behind for me. It's pretty easy to be supportive when you don't have to change anything to do it."

That made Jeanie mad, because in truth he was right—but that he'd pointed it out was just unfair as far as she could see.

"You're just jealous!" she shouted.

"Jealous? Of what?"

"That I'm going to make investigator after only a year, and it took you six."

It was as if she'd slapped him. She could literally see him shut down. Without a word he got up, picked up his discarded clothes, and went into the bathroom. Jeanie sat on the bed, tears stinging her cheeks. She knew she'd said the wrong thing, that it wasn't true, but she'd been mad and had wanted to hurt him, like he'd hurt her by not being supportive. When he emerged a few minutes later, he was dressed. He sat down on the bed and put his boots on. He didn't say a word.

When he stood and walked over to his dresser to put his holster in its place and find his keys, Jeanie said, "Donovan…"

He simply held up his hand. He grabbed his keys, clipped his badge in place, and walked out.

Donovan didn't come home that night; Jeanie didn't know where he stayed. She did her best not to worry. She was scared now; Donovan had never stayed out all night, and she knew she'd gone too far in their argument.

She slept fitfully and was awake at dawn when he walked into the bedroom. She watched as he took off his clothes and went into the bathroom. The shower started up. Lying in their bed, she wondered what to do. She wanted this chance to do investigative work. The man in personnel she'd talked to had said that maybe after a year she could transfer to the San Diego field office.

So maybe she and Donovan would have to do some kind of long-distance relationship thing. Maybe some distance would do them some good. Give them a chance to miss each other some. She purposely ignored the fact that they already had that, since they worked opposite shifts. A year really wasn't a long time, and San Francisco was only about an hour and twenty minutes away by plane. They could do this!

By the time Donovan got out of the shower, Jeanie had convinced herself it would work. She was sitting up in bed when he came out. Donovan didn't even glance at her as he walked over to the closet and pulled out clothes for the day. She watched as he dressed in black jeans and a gray sweater. It always occurred to her when she watched him that she was lucky to have him. He was handsome, sweet, considerate, funny, an excellent cook and lover, and a good friend.

"I've been thinking," she said, her voice loud in the quiet room.

Donovan didn't even look at her, sitting on the edge of the bed to put on his socks and black Doc Martens.

"Donovan," Jeanie said, her voice coaxing. "Look, I'm sorry I said what I did last night—I didn't mean it. I was mad, and it just came out."

Donovan nodded, his face still set in stone.

Jeanie took a deep breath. He wasn't going to make this easy, was he? "Okay, look, I've been thinking about it, and we can still do this. I mean, I can go to San Francisco, and we can see each other on weekends and stuff. It's only an hour and twenty minutes by plane, you know." When he didn't answer, she went on, hoping that he was actually digesting what she was saying. "I mean, right now, we don't see each other a lot anyway, right? So when we see each other we'll have lots to talk about and lots to make up time for…" She trailed off as he looked up at her, an expression of incredulity on his face.

"You've already accepted the job, haven't you?" he said.

All the hope she'd been building up crashed around her. She felt absolutely sick as she nodded slowly.

Donovan opened his mouth as if to say something, then just shook his head in disbelief. Again, he stood up without another word, picked up his badge, holster, and keys, and walked out. Jeanie lay down on the bed, knowing she'd made a mistake and not sure she could undo it even if she wanted to. It had never occurred to her that accepting the job before talking to Donovan would be construed as a betrayal. But seeing it now, through his eyes, it was. She'd accepted a job in another city and had expected him to be more than willing to move for her. After all, he could be a narc anywhere, right? She had been wrong, more wrong than she'd ever been before, and she began to wonder how much she was going to regret it.

"Sergeant Templeton?" Kyle inquired as he walked into the office.

Rhiannon turned around from her computer. "Yes, sir?"

Kyle was taken aback again by the rich green of her eyes and the haunted look they held. Did she never have a happy moment?

"Midnight asked me to come down and talk to you about working on the departmental inventory. Do you have a few minutes?" he asked.

"Of course, sir, no problem," Rhiannon said, gesturing to the chair in front of her desk and reaching for her pad and pen.

"Thank you, Sergeant." Kyle sat down, looking crisp in his black slacks and white dress shirt. "May I call you Rhiannon? 'Sergeant' is cumbersome and seems too formal to me."

"Certainly, sir," Rhiannon said, still sounding very formal.

"If it won't short your circuits out," Kyle said, smiling engagingly, "you could call me Kyle."

Rhiannon hesitated for a moment, then grinned self-consciously as she realized how militant she'd sounded. "Sorry."

"No problem," Kyle replied easily. "Now, could you tell me a little bit about the inventory program, and what your plans are?"

"Sure, sir—ah, I mean, Kyle," she said, grinning again.

She proceeded to educate Kyle on the departmental inventory, explaining in general at first, then more in depth when he questioned her further. She was amazed by his quick mind; he was able to grasp the entire process the first time she explained it, asking intelligent questions. He brought up situations that could pose problems, many of which Rhiannon herself had been grappling with.

Over the next two hours, it became very evident to Rhiannon why Kyle Masterson had been hired as the new Assistant Chief. He was intelligent, decisive, able to grasp the most intricate problem but still see the big picture. Rhiannon was impressed.

After two hours, Kyle glanced at his watch, realizing it was well into lunchtime.

"Rhiannon, I'm afraid I've infringed on your break," he said, looking chagrined.

"That's okay, sir. I don't usually go anywhere for lunch, or even eat lunch for that matter."

"You don't eat lunch?" Kyle asked, ignoring the fact that she'd called him sir again.

Rhiannon shrugged. "If I do, it's here at my desk. As you can see," she said, gesturing at the piles of paperwork around her, "I have plenty to keep me busy." It wasn't a complaint, merely a statement.

Kyle nodded, looking thoughtful. "Can I borrow your phone?"

"Certainly."

Kyle pulled out his date book, looking in the back. He dialed a number and ordered lunch for the two of them to be delivered, keeping it simple with turkey sandwiches, chips, and bottled water, with condiments on the side.

Hanging up the phone, he looked at her as she sat staring open-mouthed at him. "We have work to do."

"But, sir…" Rhiannon began helplessly.

"Teach me," Kyle said as he unbuttoned his shirt sleeves and began rolling them up.

Rhiannon looked aghast. "You're a chief!"

Kyle raised an eyebrow at her. "You think I forgot?"

"No, but… this is just simple property work, not really chief work."

"Rhiannon," Kyle said, placing his hands on the piles of paperwork and looking her straight in the eyes, "I can't do the job if I don't know the job. Teach me." His voice was beseeching, and Rhiannon couldn't help but feel grateful for what he was doing. She also couldn't help but respect a chief that was willing to get his hands dirty.

They worked until the sandwiches arrived, then Kyle insisted that they stop to eat. They moved into the break room located at the back off the office. It was a small room with a small round table and two chairs. Kyle took the time to unpack the food, setting hers in front of her along with a knife and the condiments. He even cracked the seal on her bottle of water for her. Rhiannon found this gentlemanly act endearing in a way she couldn't put her finger on.

She noted that before he started, he put a napkin in his lap, and he was very neat in how he ate. He seemed very old-world, with his polite gestures and the way that he listened to what she said then answered quietly. He didn't try to impress her; nor did he talk down to her. Kyle spoke with authority, but not authority born of rank, rather experience and intelligence. Rhiannon immediately recognized the difference. Kyle Masterson had class, a lot of it.

"Did I hear the rumor correctly?" Rhiannon ventured tentatively.

"What rumor is that?" Kyle asked, his guard coming up a bit as he wondered if she meant the one about his and Midnight's previous relationship.

"That you have two degrees from Harvard," Rhiannon said, wondering what had him looking so wary all of a sudden. As soon as she mentioned the degrees, though, he relaxed.

"Well, that's true. I have one in business administration and another in philosophy."

"Why philosophy?"

"I needed to win more debates with my wife," Kyle said, grinning.

Rhiannon laughed at that, pleasantly surprised by his answer. She had noted the wedding band he wore, but found it refreshing that a man would refer to his wife affectionately at work. Usually men in law enforcement had this rough exterior image to keep up, or at least in Kyle's case, an aloof one.

"Do you win more?" Rhiannon asked, smiling.

"I used to," Kyle said, his tone changing slightly.

"Did she get smarter on you?" Rhiannon asked without thinking, or noting the shadow that had just crossed his face.

"No," Kyle said, his voice soft now. He took a slow, deep breath and looked her directly in the eyes, knowing she'd understand. "My wife died three years ago."

Rhiannon was stunned. "Oh my God… I'm so sorry," she said, shaking her head, feeling tears sting the back of her eyes.

"It's okay," Kyle said, feeling his throat constrict a bit. "You didn't know, and I know you understand."

Rhiannon looked back at him for a long moment, then nodded slowly. She did understand. How many times had someone asked about her husband? After all, she was still wearing her wedding rings. She knew they never meant to hurt her by asking about him—how would they know, after all? But she also knew how hard it was to tell people that he was dead. Without stopping to think, Rhiannon reached across the table, placing her hand over his, looking him in the eyes.

"Yes, I do understand. Thank you for sharing that with me."

Kyle smiled weakly. "Kind of members of the same club, aren't we?"

"Yeah, we are." Rhiannon nodded. "Can I ask what happened?" she asked softly.

Kyle took a deep breath, expelling it slowly. "Breast cancer."

"That must have been very difficult," Rhiannon said sincerely.

She realized it would have been harder knowing that your loved one was going to die and not being able to do anything about it. With Jason, he'd been alive one minute and dead the next; there'd been no time to think. Of course, there hadn't been any time to say goodbye either.

"At least you got a chance to tell her that you loved her and to say goodbye, right?" Rhiannon said, putting her thoughts into words.

Kyle nodded. "I did get that. You didn't though, did you?" he asked, his voice soft and sympathetic.

Rhiannon shook her head. "No, he was killed instantly."

"It's a double-edged sword," Kyle said simply. "In every occurrence there are two sides. In every side there is an up and a down, and in every up there is a down."

"Philosophy 101?" Rhiannon asked, surprising herself with her ability to joke at a time like this.

Kyle found himself grinning. "Something like that."

They finished their lunch in companionable silence, both mulling over the fact that it had felt good to share their burdens with someone else. Maybe healing had finally started for them both.

Stevie was cooking in Rhiannon's kitchen, making meatballs for spaghetti that night. She had her radio on. No Doubt was playing, Gwen Stefani belting out, "Hey baby, hey baby, hey…" Stevie sang the words: "I'm the kinda girl that hangs with the guys, like a fly on the wall with the secret eyes. Taking it in, try to be feminine, with my makeup bag, watching all the sin." She danced to the beat as she rolled meatballs between her palms, dropping them in the sauce.

Finishing and turning with the bowl to the sink to wash it out, she danced to the chorus of the song, chanting, "All the boys say, hey baby, hey baby, hey! Girls say, girls say, hey baby, hey baby, hey! Hey baby, baaaby…"

Stevie was wearing her navy blue academy sweatpants, rolled

over a few times, bringing the top of them down over her slender hips, and a cropped tank top that exposed a fair amount of torso. It was the tanned, smooth skin that had Christian Collins mesmerized as she undulated provocatively to the song. He'd knocked on the door a couple of times, but could hear the music cranked up and knew she couldn't hear him knocking. He'd tried the door and walked in, calling out as he did. Apparently she hadn't heard him. He stood leaning against the doorjamb in the kitchen, watching her dance. There was no denying his attraction to her. She was beautiful and about as feisty as they came, and he liked it.

Stevie turned, sensing him standing there after a few moments. As the first song ended and the Latin beat of Ricky Martin's "She Bangs" started, their eyes locked for a moment and she grinned mischievously. The wench knew what she was doing! Christian shook his head, grinning back at her. Then he glanced past her at the computer desk set up at the other end of the kitchen.

"That the one?" he asked, as if he hadn't noticed her dancing a moment ago.

Stevie turned and looked at the computer, then glanced back at him. "That's the one."

Christian nodded, walking across the kitchen, his eyes flicking down at her as he passed her—her grin was still in place. He sat down and turned the computer on. He'd come over to determine if her computer needed to be upgraded, and to load the appropriate programs onto it. He was also there to install the cable modem and get her connected using the department's server.

He glanced up at the radio sitting on top of the computer desk, blasting Ricky Martin. Stevie walked over and leaned past him to turn it down. Christian got a close-up view of a very nice expanse of tanned skin, and the distinct scent of the musk that she wore. Damn! He was feeling like a bloody schoolboy again! Who was this woman, anyway? He glanced up and noticed that she was looking down at him, her eyes twinkling with mischief. She wasn't shy, that was for sure.

Stevie walked back over to the sink as Christian set to work. She was grinning to herself, knowing she'd unnerved him a bit when she'd moved so close to him. Good! Served the man right! A man didn't deserve to look as good as he did and never have a woman put him off a bit. This might be more fun than she'd realized, she thought, almost laughing to herself.

"Hey," Dave said from the kitchen doorway.

Stevie turned and looked up at him, smiling. "Hey!" she said, happy to see him.

She hadn't seen him at all in the week she'd been back at the department. She hadn't even had a chance to talk to him, he'd been so buried in work, trying to catch up from the two weeks he'd given her. He walked over and she reached up and hugged him. He hugged her back. When she pulled back, his hands remained on her hips.

Dave glanced over at Christian, who had turned around.

"Hey, Blue," Dave said, nodding to the younger man.

"Hey, Dibbs," Christian countered, his eyes gleaming with amusement, as if he'd just caught them doing something. Grinning to himself, he turned back to the computer.

Dave looked back down at Stevie, making no comment about

Christian being there. "So how's it going?"

"It's going good," Stevie said, happy to have a chance to talk to him again. She realized she'd missed his comfortable company. "Did you hear?"

"That you got a T and D? Yeah," Dave said, smiling. "Congratulations."

"Thanks," Stevie said, grimacing. "I don't think too many people are going to be too happy about it."

"Tough. Midnight made the decision—no one will question her."

"I know, but that won't stop them from hating me," Stevie said, suddenly sounding very young and unsure.

Dave pulled her into his arms, hugging her close. "They'd all grab the chance if it was offered to them, Stevie. Just do your thing, it'll all work out."

Stevie glanced up at him, smiling. He was so damned sure of everything, and it was very comforting. "Thanks," she said, feeling better all of a sudden.

It had been worrying her all week, what people were thinking and saying. But Dave was right—any of them would have snatched the chance if Midnight had offered it to them. So why shouldn't she?

She reached up then, putting her hand at the back of his neck, bringing his head down to hers, kissing him softly on the lips. He kissed her back, his arms tightening around her momentarily.

"Wanna stay for dinner?" she asked when the kiss ended.

"Can't," he said, regret in his voice. "I have a raid tonight. Maybe we can have dinner this week sometime?"

"Just let me know when—I'll be available," she said, smiling up at him.

"Just like that?" Dave asked with a grin.

"Just like that." She liked this comfortable relationship with him. It wasn't all possessive and intense, just casual and fun. She knew Dave dated a lot of women, and she didn't care, because she didn't intend to get into a committed relationship either. It was just time to relax and have fun, and that's what she intended to do. She walked Dave to the door, giving him another hug and telling him to be safe.

Christian had listened to it all, and even glanced back when they'd kissed. He had easily guessed that Dave and Stevie had a thing. He also found himself envious of the other man for the first time. He wondered if Stevie was aware of Dave's philandering ways—but then again, he didn't see Stevie O'Neil as the settling-down type either. Things were definitely going to get interesting around here.

CHAPTER 2

The same day as the bomb threat, Susan answered the door at Joe and Randy's house with her arms up over her head as she put a ponytail holder in her long blond hair. She was surprised to see Dave Dibbins standing there.

"David!" she exclaimed. "What are you doing here?" she asked, worried instantly. The only time she ever saw Dave without the rest of the gang was when there was trouble and he was there to protect her and the children.

"Oh, the usual," Dave said, grinning. "Nothing major to worry about—we're just taking some precautions."

"And you're placating me as usual," Susan said smoothly as she stepped aside to admit him into the house.

Dave's blue eyes twinkled humorously. He didn't realize she had heard him claim it was "nothing" so many times that she never believed him anymore. "I guess you've heard that before, huh?"

"Only a few dozen times," Susan said, smiling.

He grinned. "So not too many."

"Not too," Susan countered, laughing softly.

"Uncle Dave!" yelled JT as he came bounding into the room, running straight up to Dave and throwing himself into his arms as Dave knelt.

"Hey, little man, how are you?" Dave said, smiling down at the boy. Joe's son was the image of Joe himself, with dirty-blond hair cut short and light blue eyes that shined with excitement.

"Why are you here?" JT asked, cutting to the heart of the matter.

"I thought I'd drive you, Kat, and Susan to school."

"In the Charger?" JT asked excitedly.

"Would I drive anything else?"

JT squealed with joy. He loved to ride in Dave's car.

"Go get your shoes," Susan said, smiling at the boy. "Kat? Are you ready?" she called.

JT ran off to get his shoes. Out of the hallway walked Kat, Joe and Randy's daughter. She was a very pretty blend of both her parents, with Joe's blue eyes and Randy's gold-blond hair. She walked sedately up to Susan, showing her a button on her pants that she couldn't manage to fasten. Susan knelt down to help out.

Dave was just standing up, and he caught the scent of her perfume. He always liked the way she smelled, like fresh jasmine. He wondered idly what was happening with her and Christian Collins. The whole gang knew that things hadn't fallen into place for the couple. The group was divided on whether or not it was a bad thing that she hadn't ended up marrying Christian. Dave was of the opinion that if it had been real love or the right thing, it would have happened by now. Joe and he had had a couple of discussions about the matter while on surveillance or just shooting the breeze in Joe's office. Joe felt like they shouldn't rush, that if Christian needed to get the running around out of his system, it was better that he did it now, rather than marrying Susan and cheating on her.

Dave had pointed out to Joe that if Christian was in a committed relationship with Susan, sleeping with other women was still considered cheating. Of course, Joe had countered that by asking about Dave's own "girlfriend" situation, which almost always consisted of at least three girls he was seeing at a time. Dave had explained that he wasn't in what would be considered a committed relationship with any of the women, that they saw other people too. Joe had just laughed, shaking his head.

Looking at Susan now, Dave couldn't help but feel for the girl. Everyone knew that she was in love with Christian Collins; she'd left her own wedding for the man. Yet it was also common knowledge that Christian slept with anyone he pleased, while it was fairly safe to assume that Susan just sat by and waited. It just didn't seem right to Dave, but he knew it wasn't really his business. Susan was an adult, and if she chose to wait for Christian, she had the right to follow her heart.

Susan stood again, glancing up at Dave, noticing that he was looking at her. He smiled, and she smiled back. He was always very nice to her. It was so hard for her to believe that he was really this hardened narcotics officer that she understood he was. He always had such an easy smile and was very courteous. She could never equate what she'd heard he did for a living and the man that he was around her. He always reminded her of a kind of nice older brother type of person. She didn't know much about him other than that he'd been working with her aunt, uncle, and Joe for many, many years, and he was always the one that ended up at the house to protect them when there was danger brewing for the Gang. It was a comforting feeling, knowing that she was surrounded by people who knew exactly how to handle any situation.

They left for the kids' school, a private elementary school in La Jolla, a little while later. Dave let JT ride in front. Kat was quite shy, so she liked to stay close to Susan. When they arrived, Dave got out and opened the door for Susan. JT and Kat got out on the other side. They walked the kids to their respective classes then headed back to the front of the school. Once outside, a distinct cat call was heard from three young men standing off to the side of the school. They were apparently teenagers, but it was obvious they thought themselves tough guys, hanging out in their baggy jeans with knit caps pulled low on their foreheads.

"Hey, baby, who's the old man?" said one of them. Another made a lewd gesture with his tongue.

"Come here, juera. Let me show you what I got for you," said the other man, gesturing to his crotch.

Dave looked over at Susan and saw she was red-faced with embarrassment. He changed course and headed for the three boys. Susan hung back a step or two, not sure what he planned to do.

Dave was wearing his usual outfit of faded jeans, white tennis shoes, gray T-shirt tucked in, and black cotton short-sleeved shirt over it, not tucked in to cover his holstered weapon. His badge was clipped to his belt, as always, just above his right pocket and his gun. As he walked up to the young men, it was obvious they thought they were badasses; they took up aggressive, chest-pushed-out postures, their chins coming up in a veiled threat to warn the opposition they weren't the types to be messed with. Dave grinned; he dealt with tougher than this in the office.

As he drew near he swept the sides of his shirt back to not so subtly reveal the badge and gun. He smiled at the young men. "Good morning, gentlemen," he said, with overemphasized warmth. The boys had been deflated quickly by the sight of the San Diego PD badge and the rather nasty-looking weapon. Dave's apparent confidence didn't help their fast-disappearing egos either. "Now, I *know* that you weren't talking to this woman like that, right?" The last word was spoken with a steely look in his eyes.

"Uh, no, sir," said the crotch man.

"We were just messing around, sir," the tongue man said. The third remained silent, lowering his head and fidgeting.

"Good," Dave said, nodding, looking satisfied. "Because I'd hate to think that you'd be bothering my friend here."

"Come on, man," cajoled tongue man. "You gotta admit she's hot."

Dave glanced back at Susan, who stood looking distinctly mortified. He smiled and winked at her, then looked back at the young men, nodding. "She's beautiful," he agreed. "But there are a lot of ways to convey your appreciation for her appearance without being degrading, don't you think?" Then he grinned, his blue eyes twinkling. "I mean, face it—when's the last time you got a date talking to a woman like that?"

The young men all looked surprised by his comment at first, then one said, "Boo yeah!" They all laughed, nodding at what Dave was saying.

"Cool," Dave said smoothly. "So I can count on you three to be polite to the lady now, right?"

"Yeah, man, no prob," said one of the guys, putting his fist out to Dave, thumb side up. Dave followed the tradition and chucked the man's fist with his own; the man did the same back. It was the modern version of a handshake, and it was apparent that the young man was impressed that Dave knew that.

He went back to Susan then, leading her back over toward the car. Once inside she turned to him.

"Thank you for that," she said quietly.

Dave nodded. "They've been hassling you a lot, huh?"

Susan shrugged, trying to make light of it, but it was obvious that it had bothered her a lot. Then she nodded slowly, her sapphire blue eyes looking up into his, appreciation clear in them.

"Susan," Dave said, his voice soft but chiding, "anytime you have a problem like that, just let one of us know. We can always take care of stuff like that for you. Okay?"

Susan smiled in self-depreciation, shaking her head. "David, you all have much more important things to worry about than my little trials."

"Hey," Dave said, reaching out to touch her under the chin. "You're part of the family. Your trials are our trials. Okay?" He shrugged. "Hell, if nothing else, give me a call. I'm always out and about." He grinned, and Susan couldn't help but smile.

"You are too kind, David."

"No, just a sucker for a damsel in distress," he said, smiling warmly.

Susan laughed too.

They spent the next couple of weeks with him driving her and the kids to school, then taking her back to Joe's house or in some cases to the college where she was trying to finish up her degree. They talked about insignificant things—the weather, the kids, things like that. It was a companionable time though. Susan had always felt comfortable around Dave; he never made her feel ill at ease. He was so laidback, and always ready with an easy smile.

One day they were early for one of her classes, and he was too early for a connection he had, so he asked if she'd like to have coffee. She accepted.

They sat in the coffee shop, and he finally asked her how things were with Christian, not wanting to pry but curious in spite of himself.

Susan found herself telling him, just feeling the need to talk to someone about the whole situation, having gotten quite comfortable with Dave in the past two weeks.

"I just don't know… things between us are so distant right now," she said woefully.

"Right now?"

"Well, we've barely spoken for over a month." Susan didn't mention that they hadn't slept together in longer than that. Not since before he'd left for his trip to Seattle.

"What happened?" Dave asked, wanting to help if he could.

Susan shook her head. "He just needs his freedom, and I think I drag him down."

"How do you drag him down, Susan?" Dave asked, surprised at her attitude.

She shrugged, looking down at her hands. "I just think that he loves me, but can't be in a relationship without feeling like he's missing out on something else."

Dave looked at her for a long moment, then shook his head slowly. "Susan, if he really loves you, he wouldn't feel like there was anything better out there."

Susan's eyes raised to his then, and it was apparent he'd just said something she'd been trying to deny to herself for a long time.

"I'm sorry," Dave said, immediately unhappy with himself for being so blunt. He really didn't know what was in Christian's head.

"Can I ask you something?" Susan said hesitantly.

"Sure."

"I've heard that you have a lot of women in your life. I mean, I don't mean to pry, but I was just wondering if maybe you could explain why men do that…" She trailed off as her courage failed her. She felt like she was accusing him of doing something wrong when it really was none of her business. She just hoped that maybe he could explain his behavior to her, as that would help her understand Christian's. "I'm sorry," she said, feeling really foolish.

"It's okay," Dave said, grinning warmly. "Everyone knows about my love life—it's basically a departmental pastime."

Susan laughed, immediately feeling better.

"Well, I know why I don't have just one woman in my life," he said. "It may not be the reason Christian has, though, but I can explain my side. See, I want what your aunt and uncle have."

Susan nodded, understanding perfectly. She'd questioned Midnight once about what was an acceptable level of sexual attraction in a relationship. She'd always envied the very apparent love her aunt and uncle had for each other.

Dave shrugged. "Till I find the one, I'm not settling down," he said simply.

"I understand that," Susan said. She bit her lip, looking at him. "Do you think that's what Christian is doing?"

Dave grimaced, wishing she wouldn't equate his actions with Christian's. The women that he saw knew all about each other, and also dated other guys. There wasn't really a comparison, as far as he was concerned. "Susan, I don't know what Christian thinks. I just think the guy likes to play, and he's sure you'll be there when he gets done playing."

Susan looked back at him for a long moment, having never thought of it that way before. And if Dave was right, what was she doing? Exactly what Christian expected of her. That didn't sit too well with her, and it got her thinking a lot over the next few weeks about making some serious changes in the way she handled things.

The article in the *San Diego Tribune* came out a week after the incident at the high school. It ran through the department like wildfire.

Trouble in Paradise?

Rumors Abound Around Law Enforcement's Golden Girl.

Chief Midnight Chevalier has long been a respected member of the law enforcement community. Her "funeral" last year, when she was believed to have been killed, drew the eyes of the nation. All observed as

her grief-stricken husband, Richard Debenshire, mourned her, very obviously devastated by his loss. Richard and Midnight
became a household name. The country re-
joiced when Midnight Chevalier was found
alive.

Now, just over a year later, Chief Midnight
Chevalier has been accused of favoritism,
nepotism, and illegal activities. No formal complaint has been filed, but the city
council has received an anonymous letter
detailing these accusations. It is said
that Chief Chevalier promotes only people
she likes, while others with more senior-
ity wait on lists. It is also alleged that
she uses her position and the resources of
the department to protect her own family,
while leaving the streets unpatrolled during a recent standoff involving a phantom
bomb threat. Further, and most damaging of
all, it is alleged that she whitewashed
the investigation of the murder of Ramon
Calderon by a vigilante cop.

This is not the first time Midnight Chevalier and her department have been in the
spotlight. There have been many notable
appearances in the news by the charismatic
and driven Chief of Police. In years past…"

The story went on to list all the times Midnight and the department had made the news, including when Joe's own wife was charged
with the attempted murder of both Joe and Midnight. It had been a
horrendous time for all of them and had almost ended in divorce for
both Joe and Randy as well as Rick and Midnight.

Within hours of the news breaking, Midnight was inundated with calls from the media asking her to confirm or deny the allegations. Kyle was the one to bring the story to Midnight's attention first thing that morning when he got in.

"Have you seen this?" he asked, tossing the paper down on Midnight's desk. The article was circled.

Midnight scanned the story, her face changing as she read. By the time she got to the allegations she was reaching for the phone.

"Rick, get up here," she said into it.

Kyle watched as she read the rest of the article. He didn't know what was going through her head until she took the paper and flung it across the room. Rick walked in then, dodging the flying paper.

"What's wrong?" he asked, looking from Kyle to Midnight.

"That," Midnight said, pointing to the paper now lying in disarray a few inches from Rick's foot.

Rick bent down and picked it up, flipping it around to the circled part. He read the headline and then quickly scanned the rest. Kyle could see anger and incredulity on the Englishman's face. He looked up, his blue eyes sparkling with fury.

"Who the fuck…" he grated out as the door opened again.

"What the hell is this shit?" Joe asked as he strode into the office, holding his own paper aloft.

"Welcome to the party," Kyle said, crossing his arms over his chest and leaning against the table.

"Who wrote the letter?" Midnight asked, addressing no one directly.

"I don't know, but I'm sure as hell gonna find out," Rick said.

"I'll shoot the little asshole myself," Joe said.

"I second that," Dave Dibbins put in as he walked through the door with Spider on his heels.

"And I'll box him up for you," Spider said.

"As long as there's room for scorpions," Tiny Ako said as he walked in, followed closely by his wife.

Kyle watched, trying not to be amused at the growing lynch mob. He sincerely pitied the soul that had made the mistake of crossing this group.

"Who are we killing?" Kana asked, standing in the doorway. "I hope it's the little shit that wrote this letter." She held the paper in her hands as well.

Midnight couldn't help but grin at the way this was progressing. Leave it to her gang to make things better in the face of adversity. She caught Kyle's grin, hidden behind his hand as he eyed her; she shook her head, rolling her eyes.

"Okay, people, settle down," she said, standing and holding her hands up for silence.

Rick walked forward, moving to stand behind his wife. Joe went to stand on the other side of Midnight. She glanced back at both of them.

"Whoever wrote this letter obviously has a beef with me," she said, then shrugged. "Let them bring it on if they want to investigate me. I have nothing to hide."

"Are you going to respond to what this guy wrote?" Jess asked.

Midnight considered the question for a moment, then shook her head. "No, because nothing has been filed yet. This reporter is just stirring up the pot to see what flies out. It's not going to be me, or any member of my team." Her look was pointed at each of them.

Each member nodded slowly, understanding what she was saying. She wasn't going to get into a pissing match with the press. Slowly but surely the group dispersed, each going back to their own jobs. It was once again obvious to Kyle how loyal Midnight's people were to her. Throughout the day she received a number of calls as well as emails of support from members of the community. Cassandra was finally tasked with taking messages because Midnight couldn't get any work done with all the communications. It became evident too that many in the department did not support the letter writer's allegations.

Unfortunately—or perhaps fortunately—the rest of the officers in the department hadn't gotten Midnight's mandate about not talking to the press, and reporters were swarming patrol officers everywhere in the city, asking for comments.

Many of the officers supported Midnight, stating that they believed she had done a great deal for the department as a whole and for the community. There were a few that refrained from answering, and a couple that actually made negative comments about Midnight. Rick watched the news that night, seeing many of the interviews.

One officer who refused to have his name given out stated off camera that "Midnight Chevalier isn't quite the ethical cop everyone thinks she is. She's just as dirty as some of the officers she's put away."

"If I could find out who that was and get my hands on him…" Rick said, trailing off ominously, his hand balled into a tight fist.

"Richard…" Midnight said, coming out of their bathroom. She moved to sit on his outstretched legs, facing him. "You shouldn't watch this stuff."

"Why not?" he asked, staring up into her eyes as his hands slid over her arms.

"Because they're just trying to get us to react. It's a pissing contest, and no one ever wins those. Both parties just end up getting wet."

Rick pursed his lips, looking stubborn. "But that's the woman I love they're talking about."

"No," Midnight said, touching his lips. "It's Chief Chevalier they're talking about. They don't know Midnight Debenshire."

A slow grin tugged at his lips. "You know I love it when you use my name, don't you?"

Midnight nodded. "I know."

Rick sighed heavily. "This is going to get rough, you know."

Again Midnight nodded. "I know, but we've been through much worse."

"Yeah…" Rick replied, nodding slowly. The article had brought up a number of difficult memories for both of them.

"We're innocent, babe," Midnight said softly.

"I know," Rick said, looking up into her eyes again. "I love you."

Midnight leaned down, kissing his lips softly. "And I you," she whispered. They kissed for a few minutes, then Midnight moved to lie on her side next to him. Rick wrapped his arm around her, holding her close as he changed the channel on the TV.

A few minutes later there was a light knock on their door.

"Come," Rick said.

Mikeyla walked in, looking pensive. "Can I talk to you guys?"

"Sure, Keyl," Rick said, turning the TV off. "What's up?"

He sat up, as did Midnight, both watching their daughter start to pace. After a few moments she stopped and looked at them.

"That article in the paper today."

"What about it, Keyl?" Midnight asked, thinking her daughter wanted to know if the allegations were true.

"It said something about you two being estranged way back when. Doesn't that mean like getting divorced?"

Rick and Midnight were both taken aback; it was not the question either of them had been expecting.

"Yes, Keyl, that's what it means," Midnight said.

"You guys were getting a divorce once?" Mikeyla sounded stunned.

"Yeah, a long time ago," Rick said, already feeling uncomfortable with the conversation.

"Why?"

Both Rick and Midnight were confounded as to how to answer that. Midnight spoke first, trying to be honest without giving too many details.

"There was a lot going on then. I was working all the time, and it was frustrating for both of us."

"You work all the time now, Mom," Mikeyla pointed out.

Midnight glanced at Rick, her look saying, *Okay, she got me on that one.*

"Keyl," Rick began hesitantly, not sure what he wanted to tell his daughter but aware that lying wasn't an option. "I made a really big mistake."

"What did you do?" Mikeyla asked, narrowing her eyes, looking a lot like her mother at that moment.

Midnight saw the stricken look on Rick's face and turned back to their daughter. "It's not important, Mikeyla. What's important is that we got through it, and we're still together."

"What did you do, Dad?" Mikeyla asked again, her tone almost accusing now.

"Mikeyla Marie!" Midnight gasped, even as Rick answered their daughter.

"I had an affair," he said, his voice stronger than he would have believed it could be.

"You had an affair?" Mikeyla repeated, dumbfounded. "How could you?"

"Hey," Midnight interceded. "Before you go off on your father, you should know I had one too, so he's not the guilty party here."

Mikeyla's eyes widened. "Why didn't I know about all this?"

"We didn't see the point in telling you," Midnight said. "It was past history, and not important to our lives now."

"But the whole world knows it now!" Mikeyla said, her concerns coming to bear.

"Yeah," Rick said. "And they also know that I love your mother very much, and that she loves me enough to have stayed with me through everything."

"Why do you two have to be so famous?" Mikeyla asked, her tone a sneer.

"We never asked to be," Midnight replied tiredly.

"But you are. Why?"

Rick sighed deeply. "Mikeyla, what your mother has done in her career is astounding. What she's done to turn her life around and affect so many other people and change their lives like she has is nothing short of a miracle. People see that, and they want to be part of it, even if it's to report it." He leaned forward, kissing Midnight's temple. "Even if it's just to stand on the sidelines and watch, and even if it's just to love her as much as he possibly can, and pray he can keep her with him forever."

Midnight had to swallow against the sudden lump in her throat.

"Mikeyla," she began, her voice coming out unsteadily at first, to the point that she had to clear her throat. "The people your dad and I work with are pretty dynamic people—they do everything with passion and intensity. That captures people's attention. I'm sorry if that's making things difficult for you right now. But honestly, honey, the work that these people do is important, and they need to do it the way they do, and if it grabs headlines or causes some stir, then that's what happens."

"People are saying that you're a dirty cop and you shouldn't be chief," Mikeyla said, her voice smaller now.

"Your mother is the best damned cop this city has, and she is also best chief this department has ever had," Rick said. "Crime is at an all-time low in this city, and morale in the department is at an all-time high. That's been since your mother took over. So you go back to those people who are saying that, and tell them that. If they still say she's dirty, then they don't know their asses from a hole in the ground."

Midnight grinned at the last comment. "Keyl, I haven't done anything wrong or illegal. There are just people in the department that don't think like I do, and one of those people wrote a very angry letter full of accusations. That's all they are. Reality as that person sees it. That doesn't mean he or she is right. Okay? Don't believe everything you read, honey. It's always from one person's point of view. It's up to you to look at the facts as you know them and weigh them against what you're reading. You know me."

Mikeyla nodded, swallowing hard. "You're right. I know you wouldn't do any of that stuff that letter said. I'm sorry, Mom."

"It's okay," Midnight said, holding her arms out to her daughter. Mikeyla climbed onto the bed, hugging her mother. Then she looked up at Rick, still sitting behind Midnight.

"I'm sorry, Dad."

Rick gave her a stern look, spoiled by the slow grin that started on his lips. "Just don't let it happen again." He leaned down and kissed her on the head.

Ricky found them still hugging ten minutes later, and climbed onto the bed to join in. The three of them laughed as they hugged him too.

***

Things with Donovan and Jeanie weren't getting any better. Usually they tried to at least have dinner together before Jeanie reported for her graveyard shift, but the evening after Donovan stayed out all night, he again didn't come home. When she got home from her shift the next morning, she found that he was dressed and ready to leave when she walked in. He left without saying a word to her. Overnight they'd become strangers. It terrified her. She talked to Erin about it a few days later while they had lunch.

"I don't know what to do to fix it," Jeanie said, after telling Erin the whole story.

"I'm sorry things aren't going well," Erin put in, not sure what to say.

She couldn't honestly understand why Jeanie was taking the chance of losing Donovan over this career move. But then again, Erin realized that she didn't have quite the drive that Jeanie did. At least not where a career was concerned. Erin was realistic, too; she knew that just because she had a hang-up about finding true love, it didn't mean that love was as important to everyone. Jeanie was her friend, though, and she wanted to try and be supportive.

Jeanie had confided in Erin during the whole process with Alcoholic Beverage Control. Erin hadn't thought the idea of not telling Donovan was a good one. She had pointed that out to Jeanie, but Jeanie had told her that the chances of her actually getting on were so slim, she didn't see the point in freaking Donovan out ahead of time for nothing.

"So what are you going to do?" Erin asked, worried.

She had begun to care a lot about both of them, and thought their love affair was so romantic; she hated to see anything happen to it. She also knew that Jeanie was far more independent and single-minded than she herself could ever be.

Jeanie shook her head. "I don't know. I've got a week till I have to report to the academy."

"Then what?"

"I guess I'll have to see if he misses me."

"Jeanie!"

"Hey, he's not even trying here. He's just sitting back, waiting for me to change my mind," Jeanie said, sounding hurt.

"Maybe you should try talking to him again," Erin suggested hopefully.

"He's never around long enough for me to talk to," Jeanie said sourly.

"You have a night off tonight, right?"

"Yeah," Jeanie said, sounding reluctant to give in at all.

"You have to try, Jeanie," Erin said, her voice holding her concern for their romance. "He loves you, you love him. You need to try one more time."

Jeanie looked thoughtful for a minute, then sighed heavily. "You're right, I need to try."

That night she waited for Donovan to come home. He was usually back by six o'clock. Six came and went; so did seven, eight, nine, and ten. He finally walked in at 11:30. Jeanie was in their room by then, lying on the bed, still fully clothed. She sat up. He didn't say anything.

"Are we ever going to talk again?" Jeanie asked, her frustration obvious.

Donovan didn't answer for a long moment as he took off his holstered weapon and unclipped his badge, laying both on his dresser. Finally he turned around, crossing his arms in front of his chest and leaning back against the dresser.

"What would you like to talk about, Jay?" he asked, his voice far from amenable.

"This," Jeanie said, shaking her head at his attitude. "Us."

His face took on a cynical look. "I thought you'd already decided *this* for *us*."

"I didn't say I wanted to never talk to you again. You made that decision on your own," Jeanie said stridently.

"Yeah. Guess I got to make one decision about this, huh?"

"Donovan, this doesn't have to be the end of us."

"Sure feels like an end when my fiancée moves across the state without even talking to me about it first."

"I told you why I didn't tell you."

"Yeah, you told me."

"And you can't forgive that?"

"No, Jay, what I can't forgive is making the decision without even having the decency to be honest with me about it from the beginning. You out and out lied to me—that's a lot more than just trying to spare me some worry."

"Okay, so I made a mistake. I should have told you from the beginning," Jeanie agreed. "Why can't we get past this?"

"You're moving four hundred miles away."

"You've never heard of long-distance relationships?"

"Yeah, I've heard of them," Donovan said, his tone no-nonsense. "I never wanted one."

"It might only be for a year. Then I can probably transfer to the San Diego office."

"Call me when that happens," Donovan said cynically.

"So that's just it?" Jeanie asked incredulously.

Donovan didn't answer, simply looked back at her for a long moment. "I didn't make this decision, Jeanie. You did."

"Yes, I decided to make a career move."

"Yeah, and you decided to make that move four hundred miles away from me."

Jeanie just stared at him for a long moment. Slowly she reached up and pulled the diamond ring off her left ring finger. With tears in her eyes, she got off the bed, walked over to him, and leaned past him to place it on top of his badge. She turned and left the room.

Donovan heard the front door close a few minutes later. He stood frozen at his dresser, staring down at the ring he'd given her three years before. He couldn't believe it had been that simple for her to give it up. He had no way of knowing that she was even then crying hysterically in her car, down the street from the house they shared.

Jeanie went to Erin's place, a three-bedroom house she shared with two other people. Jeanie slept on the couch. Erin did her best to console her friend, stunned that Jeanie had actually taken her ring off and given it back to Donovan. This was not the way things were supposed to go! She had no idea what to say. She was upset that things had gotten so bad between them so quickly. Erin had sincerely hoped that talking tonight would help them.

The next morning, around 9:00, Jeanie got up and went back over to the house. Donovan's car was not in the driveway. In their bedroom, she noticed that the ring was still on Donovan's dresser. She took most of her clothes and all of her uniforms and equipment, walking out of the house two hours later with a sense of unreality.

She was actually leaving Donovan. There was a sick feeling in her stomach, but she knew it was too late to go back now. She'd made her decisions, and now she was going to have to stick with them, for better or worse. She moved back home that day, with no real explanation to her family other than that she was moving to San Francisco to take a new job.

A week later, she left for Huntington Beach. She drove by the house she'd lived in with Donovan. She cried all the while, as she'd done many nights since she'd moved out. She noticed that even though it was noon on a weekday, his car was in the driveway. She kept driving. She didn't know that he was passed out in the house, on their bed. He'd been drunk a lot since he'd come home to find her things gone. It was taking everything he had to hold it together while on the job.

Things with his undercover case were coming to a head, and he knew he needed to be careful. He pushed the feelings of exhaustion down deep while he was working, but the effort was making him sick. Within a week he was throwing up blood regularly. Erin got to witness it first-hand, when she came to see him two weeks after Jeanie had left town.

She buzzed the door, and after hearing it was her, Donovan let her in. She came down the hallway and heard the most horrible retching. She walked in to see him throwing up in the sink. There was blood, a lot of it.

"Donovan!" she exclaimed, terrified that he'd been injured. "Are you okay?" she asked as she touched his back.

Donovan nodded, his hands braced on either side of the sink, as he fought the waves of nausea. After a few minutes, he rinsed his mouth out, drying it with a towel. Then he moved slowly, almost painfully past Erin back to his bed. He sat down, looking years older. Since he wore no shirt, Erin couldn't help but notice that he had lost weight; his stomach was almost hollowed out now.

She sat next to him, looking at him in concern.

"Are you sick?" she asked gently.

Donovan grinned sardonically. "In a way."

"Donovan…" Erin said, her tone motherly.

Donovan closed his eyes, shaking his head. "I'm okay, Erin. I just need to get a handle on things."

Erin gave him a long, searching look, and his teal eyes met hers. She could see the sadness in them, and it made her want to cry. She leaned forward, putting her arms around him. Donovan leaned against her as she stroked his back.

"I'm sorry this happened," she said, feeling tears sting the backs of her eyes. Donovan just nodded.

They stayed that way for a while. Eventually, Donovan sat up, looking a bit better. He turned on the TV and they both sat back against the headboard. After a little while, Erin got up and went to his kitchen. She made him some tea and toast, and brought it back into the bedroom and handed it to him without a word. Donovan looked at the food, grimacing.

"Eat, Donovan. You have to keep your strength up," she said gently.

Donovan gave her a cynical look.

"Don't give me that look, Curtis. Just eat," she said, giving him a look that very much resembled a mother scolding her child. Donovan couldn't help but grin.

He ate some of the toast and drank some of the tea. They watched TV, flipping around the channels until they came to a movie they both liked. After a while, Donovan moved to lie down, his head bumping her arm. Erin reached over and stroked his hair. His eyes closed immediately.

She sat watching him as he slept. This was far from what she'd imagined would happen when she saw him again. She had been sure he wouldn't want to see her, since she'd been Jeanie's friend and basically a party to what Jeanie had hidden from him. She'd been surprised when he'd let her in. She was very happy right then that he was allowing her to be his friend too.

When Donovan woke later that afternoon, he asked her to stay for dinner. He made them a light meal, and they ate quietly. She noticed he seemed to have lost a lot of his zest for life. It bothered her to see him so devastated. She'd hoped that he would be okay; she didn't like to see people hurting, and she found herself a little angry at Jeanie for doing this to him. She had told herself that a guy like Donovan wouldn't be down for long, but it was obvious he was desolate over what had happened. The way Jeanie had told it, he was fine with the whole thing. Of course, he may have put that act on for Jeanie, to keep her from seeing him hurting too.

That evening, when she left Donovan's house he hugged her and thanked her for being there. She left happy that she had taken the chance to come and see him that day. She also made a mental note to check on him more often, since it was obvious that he needed someone keeping an eye on him.

Things had been quiet. Almost too quiet, Rick thought, as far as Julio Martinez was concerned. But after two weeks with nothing happening, they started to relax.

"Maybe the show of force at the school scared the shit out of him," Spider pointed out.

Rick shook his head. But later that night, when he mentioned Spider's comment to Midnight, she agreed. "Julio is a coward," she said derogatorily. "Any man who has to hit a woman to feel like a man is a coward."

She remembered well the day she'd met Julio Martinez. She and Donovan had been down in Mexico to find a hit man who had tried to kill Randy Curtis. They'd been having lunch in a cantina when there was a ruckus, a man attacking his wife. The man had been Julio Martinez; his wife, Marta, had been Ricardo's mother. Midnight had made a connection with Ricardo a few minutes before Julio entered the cantina. When Julio made a gesture indicating he intended to hit his wife, Midnight interceded, besting Julio and his blustering ego easily. Neither Midnight nor Julio had known who the other was then. They'd had no idea that it was Midnight who the couple had been fighting about, just some jefe de policía from San Diego. Nor had Midnight known that Julio Martinez had been hired by some dirty cops in her own department to kill her.

It had been fate. Marta Martinez had been so grateful to the petite blond police officer that she'd been horrified to find out about her husband's latest "job." It was Marta who had pushed Midnight out of the way when the car bomb set by Julio went off. It was Marta who had been killed by the bomb, and whose body had been mistaken for Midnight's. Marta had been the brave one in the family, and she'd died saving Midnight's life.

"Well, he may be a coward," Rick said, leaning down to kiss her lips softly, "but I'd feel a lot better if he was back in custody."

"Me too," Midnight admitted. It wasn't their safety they were concerned for, but Ricardo's and now Mikeyla's. Julio had made it apparent that he intended to not only take his son back, but exact some sort of revenge on Midnight. He'd also shown that he didn't have a problem with taking that revenge through an innocent child.

The following evening, Rick decided to take them all out for dinner. They needed a break from the tension. They went to an Italian restaurant that they all liked where Midnight knew the owners; the service was good, and so was the food. They spent two hours just laughing and talking. Rick and Midnight shared a bottle of red wine. It was a nice, relaxing evening. They walked out of the restaurant into the chilly night air still talking about inconsequential things. Rick and Midnight were holding hands as they headed to Rick's Saleen Mustang. It was his latest acquisition in the sporty American muscle cars he preferred. He'd bought it outright with some of his trust fund money. Midnight had asked him when she was being replaced with the twenty-year-old girlfriend. Rick had laughed and said that she was irreplaceable. Midnight had chided him that he would probably trade her in on two twenty-year-olds and get change. Rick had laughed at that.

They were about twenty feet from the car when a man stepped from the shadows. Rick pulled up instantly, his sixth sense telling him there was danger before the man even stepped into the street light. Midnight was slightly behind him and to his left; he started tugging

57

her hand to pull her farther behind him as he recognized Julio Martinez and saw the fairly nasty-looking gun in his hand. Rick felt Midnight tense, and knew that she'd realized what was going on too.

Rick held up his hand in a deflecting gesture. His right hand was down at his side, but his fingers worked as he prepared to draw the gun from the shoulder holster under his left arm.

"I want my son," Julio said in heavily accented English. "And your bitch of a wife dead," he added, grinning maliciously.

"That's not going to happen," Rick said calmly.

"I can kill you too, pendejo."

Rick felt rather than saw Midnight gesturing for the kids to get down. Her hand was still in his and he was still trying to pull her behind him, but she was fighting him, wanting a clear shot if she got a chance.

"Don't move!" Julio yelled, as if sensing what Rick was doing. "I'll fucking kill you both, and your brat too."

"Put the gun down, Julio," Midnight said. "You'll never get away with it—you're in my town now. You'll never make it to the border before my people hunt you down and kill you."

"We'll just see," Julio said, and without warning fired his gun.

In that split second, Rick stepped in front of Midnight, yanking her back at the same time and reaching up to draw his gun. There were two more shots fired on top of each other, and Julio fell. Ricardo and Mikeyla both screamed, not able to see what was happening because they were down on the ground.

When Mikeyla looked up, she saw that both her mother and father had drawn their weapons, and were still holding them out in front of them, the barrels smoking. Julio Martinez was on the ground. Then, as she watched, her father sank to his knees.

"Rick!" Midnight yelled, making a grab at him to keep him from hitting the pavement.

"I'm okay," Rick said hoarsely.

Midnight knelt in front of him. She immediately saw the scarlet stain starting at his waistline. "Jesus..." she breathed, glancing behind him and seeing Mikeyla getting up and helping Ricardo up. "Mikeyla, go inside and tell them to call the police. Take Ricardo with you," she said in the calmest voice she could muster.

"But Mom..."

"Just do it, Mikeyla!" Midnight yelled. "Please," she added, trying to hold it together.

Mikeyla nodded reluctantly and turned with Ricardo to run back to the restaurant.

Midnight immediately reached into her jacket and pulled out her cell phone, dialing 911. She moved cautiously to check Julio Martinez for a pulse; he didn't have one that she could detect, and she kicked the gun out of his now limp hand.

"This is Chief Chevalier. I need an ambulance at 2120 Mission Gorge Road, an officer is down. Get them here now!"

"Yes, ma'am!" the dispatcher responded instantly.

Midnight dropped her phone, looking at her husband, who was watching her.

"Is he dead?" Rick asked. His voice was weaker, which scared her.

She nodded, moving to his side. "Rick, I'm gonna sit you down,

59

okay?"

"I can do it," he said.

"Okay—slow, babe, slow."

He moved slowly, propping himself up against a nearby vehicle. His gun was still in his hand, and he looked at it calmly, as if wondering where it had come from. Midnight realized he was probably going into shock. She prayed for the ambulance to move faster. She ran over to his car, pulled out the first aid kit, and ran back to him. She dropped down on her knees next to him. Pulling out the pressure pad, she set it aside, then pulled his shirt carefully out of his jeans to find the point of bleeding; it was just above his belt. Putting a steel vice on her anxiety, she pressed a pad to the wound. Rick flinched visibly.

"I'm sorry, babe," Midnight said softly. "I gotta do this."

"I know," he said, his voice pained.

Midnight glanced up to make sure Mikeyla and Ricardo were inside the restaurant. She didn't really want to have them see Rick like this. She knew it would upset Mikeyla a great deal, and probably Ricardo too, although it was less likely the young boy would understand as easily.

"Come on, come on…" Midnight chanted under her breath, trying to hurry the ambulance by sheer will. She clenched her teeth to keep from losing her cool. *He's fine*, she told herself. *He's talking and coherent, he's fine*. To him, she said, "Stay with me, babe."

"I'm here," he said, his voice strained. She could see, looking into his eyes, that he was in great pain.

What she couldn't see was that he was using every ounce of

strength he had to stay alert. He knew that she'd lose it right now if he went out, and he didn't want to do that to her. He kept telling himself over and over again that at least it was him, and not her or one of the kids. That was his last thought as he finally lost the battle with unconsciousness, that at least the bastard hadn't taken his wife again. Rick didn't hear Midnight scream at him, or see the tears as she got on the phone again, yelling at the 911 operator, asking where the hell the ambulance was.

Rick woke in a hospital bed. The first face he saw was that of his life-long friend Joe Sinclair.

"Ugh," Rick said, giving him a sour look.

"What?" Joe replied, grinning already.

"Your mug is the last thing I wanna see after coming back from the brink of death," Rick said jovially.

"Yeah," Joe said, smiling. "You're fine."

"Am I?" Rick asked, sure that he was too. He was in pain, but not too much, and everything seemed normal.

"Yeah, took one in the gut, but you'll be good to go in a couple of days." Joe gave his friend a quizzical look. "What made you think you were bulletproof?"

"Huh?"

"We heard what happened—you stepped in front of Midnight as the guy fired," Joe said informatively.

"Maybe it was an accident."

"And maybe you're full of shit," Joe said, his tone no-nonsense. "You just took a bullet for your wife."

Rick's lips twitched. Then he took a deep breath, expelling it slowly, realizing it hurt to do so. "Hurt like hell too."

"Good," Joe said, without any mercy in his voice. "Maybe that way you won't pull a dumbass stunt like that again."

"You'd rather he'd shot Midnight?" Rick countered, raising an eyebrow at his best friend, who also happened to be best friends with Midnight.

"No," Joe replied, narrowing his eyes at Rick. "I'd rather you'd both remembered to duck and cover like you were taught."

Rick grinned, knowing Joe was attempting to chastise him for something that he himself would have done. "Sir, yes, sir," he said, giving his friend a mock half-salute with two fingers. "I'll remember that, sir."

"Damned well better," Joe growled, having to get the last word. "Now, the next order of business."

"Where's Night?" Rick asked before Joe could move on.

"She'll be here soon—she went to make sure the kids are okay and to take care of the report. Not before she was told that you were fine, however."

"And Martinez?"

"Dead."

"Good," Rick said, without remorse.

"Now, as I was saying," Joe went on, "there's a reporter here that wants to talk to you."

"Joe," Rick said, giving his friend a sour look, "you know I don't talk to reporters."

"Yeah, well, you might wanna talk to this one." Joe rubbed the bridge of his nose with his forefinger. "He's the one that wrote that story on Midnight and that letter."

Rick's eyes narrowed. "Where's my gun?"

"Easy now," Joe said, grinning, though he understood his friend's desire to kill the reporter. "The guy says he wants to get your side, that he tried to get a statement from Midnight's office and they said 'no comment.'"

"That's Midnight's standard answer, man, you know that. She doesn't get into pissing contests."

"Yeah." Joe nodded. "But I think she needs to do something about this one. Her credibility will take a big hit if she doesn't respond."

Rick looked at his friend for a long moment, then finally nodded. "Alright, go get him—quick, before I change my mind."

Joe led a man into the room. He was short and balding, and introduced himself as Ron Tripps. He stepped forward, extending his hand to Rick. Rick took it, his eyes wary.

"I appreciate you meeting with me, Lieutenant Debenshire."

"Just make it quick," Rick said gruffly.

Tripps nodded, understanding Rick's attitude. "How are you doing?"

"I'm alright," Rick responded, not giving him anything.

"And your family is alright?"

"Yeah, they're fine," Rick said, becoming impatient. "Is this what you wanted to talk about?"

Tripps inclined his head, realizing Rick Debenshire wasn't one to be soothed by considerate words. "Lieutenant, I know that you're probably upset about the article—"

"Upset?" Rick interrupted. "No, I'm not upset. I'm pissed—there's a difference."

"Sir, I tried to get a statement from your wife's office."

"Well, you shouldn't have just run with what you had. Her career is on the line here."

"I tried to get her side."

"You didn't try hard enough," Rick said simply.

It was obvious to Tripps he wasn't going to win. "What happened tonight?" he asked, changing subjects.

Rick had just started to answer him when Midnight walked in.

"Richard Joshua Debenshire, what the fuck did you think you were doing?" she practically shouted as she strode into the room.

Rick grimaced, knowing she'd been talking to Joe. "Midnight, this is Ron Tripps," he said by way of a distraction.

Midnight nodded in the man's direction, but never took her eyes off her husband.

"What were you thinking?" she asked again, her eyes searching his.

Rick took a deep breath, winced because it hurt to do so, then said, "I couldn't let him take you from me again."

It was a simple statement, but it spoke volumes. Tripps sat quietly, not wanting to interrupt the poignant moment between the two. It was a pretty well-known fact that Rick Debenshire was deeply in love with his wife. Anyone who had witnessed the funeral the year before knew that. But to step in front of a bullet and risk his own life for her? This was the stuff movies were made out of, that books were written about; it was true, deep, abiding love. Tripps started jotting down notes on his pad.

"I can't lose you, Rick," Midnight said, reaching out to touch his cheek. "I'd die without you too."

Rick reached up, covering her hand with his and pressing it against his cheek. "I'm still here, babe."

"Yeah, but you didn't know you would be when you stepped in front of that bullet, Richard," Midnight said, her tone more stern this time.

"It's no worse than what you did in Mexico," Rick pointed out mildly, not wanting to get into a fight over this. He was referring to the time a drug dealer had had him cornered and was holding a gun on him. Rick had dropped his weapon, but it was obvious the man planned to kill him anyway. Midnight had come up from the side and leaped in between them, shooting at the man just as the dealer fired.

Midnight gave him a narrowed look. "Don't start with me. You know what I did was a calculated risk."

"That could have gotten you killed."

"I had a vest on," Midnight said tightly.

"He could have hit you in that hard head of yours—moot point for a vest there, love."

Midnight narrowed her gold-green eyes at him again, knowing he was right but also that he had taken a much bigger chance than she had years before.

Rick reached out, putting his hand behind her neck and pulling her to him, wincing as he did. He kissed her lips softly. "I love you," he whispered against them.

Midnight held out an extra two beats before whispering, "And I you."

"Now..." Rick said, his voice trailing off as he looked over at Tripps again.

"Oh, shit," Midnight said, just then remembering there was someone else in the room with them. She turned to Tripps. "Hi. Who are you again?"

Ron stood up, extending his hand to Midnight. "Ron Tripps, *San Diego Tribune*."

"The one that wrote the story," Rick put in smoothly.

Midnight's eyes narrowed again, and Ron Tripps suddenly felt the heat of her anger pointed in his direction. Tripps glanced at Rick and found the Englishman staring back at him with an "I told you so" look on his face.

"Ma'am, please understand..." Tripps began hesitantly.

"Don't worry about it," Midnight said, waving his explanations away. "What do you want from me now?"

Ron Tripps found that it was hard not to feel nervous in her presence. She did wield a lot of power in this town, and he had allowed himself to write a story that made her look pretty bad, and he really hadn't tried *that* hard to get a comment from her. It was a piece of sensationalism, something he wasn't normally given to doing. Now he was facing the music.

"I'd like your side of the story, Chief Chevalier."

"Ask me questions."

"The allegation of unfair promotions," Ron started, his voice quavering just a little. "Have there been people, friends of yours, promoted before other deserving officers?"

"That's two questions," Midnight said, her tone still icy. "One, yes, people have been promoted, and two, yes, some of them were my friends. When you work in a department for twenty years, Mr. Tripps, you end up with a lot of people you consider friends. But were the friends that have been promoted less deserving than any other officer in the department? The answer would have to be no. I promote people who do their job, do it right, and do it well. Whether or not they are friends of mine doesn't matter."

Ron Tripps nodded, already feeling like he'd taken on more than he could handle. "What about the allegations of misusing the department's resources?"

"The resources of this department were utilized by me for the protection of an entire middle school. The fact that my daughter goes to that school, and indeed was the direct target, doesn't negate the fact that the man was threatening to bomb the entire school."

Ron Tripps nodded again, not having realized that it had been a bomb threat, only that Chief Chevalier's daughter had been threatened. He was all ready to horsewhip his assistant for not getting all the facts before he'd gone to press.

"What about the worst allegation, of whitewashing a murder investigation for one of your officers?"

Midnight was silent for a minute, debating how much she could safely tell this man without putting Stevie O'Neil in danger. "Forensics found it a clear case of self-defense. The officer in question's own account of the incident fully supports the evidence found at the crime scene. The man was attempting to attack her, and when he refused to abandon his notion of doing so, my officer fired. She was within her rights to kill the man with her first shot, since he was coming at her with a weapon and he was twice her size, but she decided to use less than reasonable force to attempt to keep from killing him. What she did was not only not criminal, it was a highly admirable display of respect for life. That type of control should be celebrated, not discouraged."

Again Tripps was taken aback. Midnight Chevalier was not someone he wanted to tangle with verbally. He knew that she held a degree in law, and thought she would make one hell of a lawyer.

"Chief Chevalier, who do you think wrote that letter? And for what purpose?" he asked, wanting to know what she thought of this person's betrayal.

"I don't know who wrote it," Midnight said calmly. Rick was still holding her hand as he watched her talk. "I have learned, though, that you can please some of the people some of the time, but never all of the people all of the time. As far as I'm concerned, if the person doesn't like the way things are done, and they don't want to come to me about their issues, then they can just get the hell out of my department." Her green eyes sparked fire, and Tripps was fairly sure she meant every word.

"Can people come to you with grievances?" he asked. "I mean, directly to you?" Tripps knew all about the chain of command within any business, and he'd heard it was more so for law enforcement.

"I have an open-door policy. I always have, and always will."

"Yes, Chief, but officials say that all the time, and they don't really," Tripps said, his tone slightly chiding.

"Ask her people," Rick put in warningly. He didn't like anyone doubting Midnight's word. He knew how personally she took her job, and how much she did to try and ensure that her officers, all of them, were taken care of on a daily basis.

"I'll do that," Tripps said, standing and extending his hand to Rick, and then to Midnight. "Thank you for your time. I'm glad everything turned out alright tonight."

"Thanks," Rick said.

"You're welcome," Tripps said, looking at Midnight. "Chief, I wonder if you'd ever be open to the idea of a ride-along."

"For you?"

"Yes, sort of a day-in-the-life kind of thing."

"Nobody wants to hear about my boring life, Tripps," Midnight said, rolling her eyes. "Stick to the ambulance chasing, it's more exciting to read."

Tripps grinned, catching her subtle jab but thinking he'd like to pursue the idea. He also knew that he was getting a rare opportunity here, meeting her in person and getting to spend this much time in her and her husband's presence. It was a unique experience. He'd seen a lot about the dynamic Chief of Police for San Diego PD, but this had been his first opportunity to meet her.

"Chief, I think you underestimate your fame in this town," he said.

"Tripps, I think you overestimate my need to be famous in this town," Midnight replied, smiling to take the bite out of her words.

"She'll think about it," Rick said, a grin playing at his lips, even as his wife gave him a dirty look.

"I will?" she asked cynically.

"Yes, you will," Rick said seriously.

"And I'd do that why?" Midnight asked, not intimidated by his tone at all.

"Because you need these people to support you to do your job, Midnight, and you don't need to take shit like this lying down anymore."

"Rick, the people that hate me will always hate me. I'm not kissing anyone's ass to get them to change their mind."

"And I'm not asking you to. I'm suggesting that people would better understand how hard you work if they got a chance to read all that you do."

"Not my style," Midnight said dismissively.

Rick took a deep breath, groaning at having done so, because it hurt. "For once in your bloody life," he said, his voice a loud whisper, "could you just not be difficult?"

"Would you love me if I changed now?" Midnight asked sweetly, the beginnings of a grin on her lips.

"Try me, just once," Rick said, grinning too.

Tripps couldn't help but smile. He was seeing quite easily why people were enchanted by these two. They were magnetic, making a person want to stay near them in hopes that their charisma and attraction would rub off. That was the impression Ron Tripps left the hospital room with that night.

CHAPTER 3

In order for Stevie to get started working the chat room angle, it became necessary for her and Christian to go out and purchase her a notebook, since she'd often need to be with him to be able to more easily coordinate what and who they'd target in the chat room. They left the office, Christian saying he'd drive. Like a lot of men, he didn't like to be a passenger. Stevie agreed, curious what a man like Christian Collins would drive. Since her father and brother-in-law, the two most influential men in her life, had been major car buffs, Stevie found that she judged men a lot by the kind of car they drove. She herself had a brand new Pontiac Trans Am that had blown the doors off a number of cars whose drivers had challenged her.

She was not disappointed when they stopped at a Dodge Viper GTS. She was a bit surprised, actually. Stevie knew how much Vipers cost, since she'd have loved to have one herself but couldn't afford it. Christian's was a rich sapphire blue with a black leather interior. *An expensive player's car*, was the thought that came to Stevie's mind, and she knew Christian Collins was a player, big time. His body language, sure grin, and cocky attitude screamed it on an almost a constant basis. Stevie had yet to see him unsure of himself, and she seriously doubted she ever would.

"Nice," she said as she slid into the passenger's seat, surprised again that he'd opened and held the door for her.

Christian grinned. "Thanks."

He got in on the driver's side and turned the ignition. The car started with a very pleasant growl.

Stevie had always been seduced by the sound of a powerful engine. She was sure it was at least part of her attraction to Dave, with his classic Charger. To her, the car was indeed an extension of a man's personality. Dave's car was very much him, a classic and understated but powerful as all get out, whereas Christian was flashy, cocky, definitely hot, but also compelling in his own way.

She'd rarely, if ever, denied herself anything or anyone she thought she wanted. She figured in this day and age women had just as much right to take the initiative as men did, so she often did. In this case, though, she was fairly sure Christian Collins could hold his own on the hard-to-hold gauge. And for once she wasn't altogether sure she wanted to tempt such a fate.

Usually, men were basically passing fancies to her; she didn't stay with any for very long, because they usually started to try controlling her too soon. No one controlled Stevie O'Neil. Anyone who tried was summarily dismissed. There hadn't been an incident of Stevie getting burned since she'd been in high school. She still remembered it, and had no intention of repeating the mistake or the rejection.

Christian Collins was the kind of man that could reject her flat out and not bat an eyelash. She didn't plan to find out if he would. She also refused to acknowledge that despite all of this, she was seriously intrigued by this man, as she imagined most women were. It was like looking in a magazine and seeing this gorgeous man staring out of the pages at you. Looking into his eyes and for one fleeting moment wondering what he was like. Was he good in bed? Was he kind? Was he tender? Did he do romantic things? Or was he an asshole? Was he conceited? Or rude? The curiosity was never satisfied, because obviously you'd never meet the guy in the magazine. But here he was, right here, flesh and blood. It was a lot harder to deny the desire when it was so temptingly close at hand. How long could she resist?

"So," she said, shoving aside all her thoughts. "This is a ten-cylinder, right?"

"Yes," Christian said, grinning in bemusement. He was surprised that a woman would know cars at all, let alone engine sizes.

Stevie nodded. "So what liter capacity then?"

Again he grinned, wider this time. "8.0."

"Wow, this thing kicks ass," Stevie said, not hiding her admiration.

"That's the idea," Christian said as he pulled out of the parking lot.

They drove in silence for a while.

"This is a lot of money to drop on a car. You must make a lot as a computer geek," Stevie said.

Christian gave her a dirty look. "It's hacker—get the label right."

Stevie laughed. "Okay, they pay you hackers real well."

"Actually, most of this car was bought with a check I had from another source."

"Another source? Sounds mysterious."

Christian laughed. "Not so mysterious. Someone sold a car I had in England for $55,000 and sent me the check."

"Damn!" Stevie said, giving a low whistle of appreciation "They buy cars for a lot in England, huh?"

Christian pursed his lips, knowing she was teasing him. "It was a Jaguar XK8."

"Oh," Stevie replied simply, looking repentant. "Nice car too."

"Yup," Christian replied, not sure why he'd found it necessary to tell her how he'd afforded the Viper. "So," he said after a long silence, "what do you drive?"

"Trans Am," she supplied, watching for his reaction. A Trans Am was definitely a modern muscle car, not something "ladies" usually drove. She was curious to see what he'd say.

Christian narrowed his eyes. "Eight-cylinder, 5.8 liter, right?"

"Yes, sir," Stevie said, grinning. He didn't have problems with women having power, apparently.

He nodded. "Nice."

There was another long silence. The radio was on and Christian frequently reached over to change the channel. When one song ended, he'd look for another he liked. Judging from the songs he settled on, he liked a pretty wide variety of music. At one point he stopped on hip-hop artist Nelly's "#1." The chorus went, "What does it take to be number one? Two is not a winner and three nobody remembers." Christian seemed to know every word, and Stevie found that the song seemed to fit his personality. At one point the lyrics said, "I'm like Sprint or Motorola, no service, out of your range." She wondered if that was true too.

Again she realized she wanted to find out. God! What was with this guy? Sure, he was movie star handsome, but that wasn't usually something that caused this kind of attraction for Stevie. She had heard a lot about him though. She knew that he'd been key in taking down Devereaux and the other dirty cops who tried to have Midnight Chevalier killed. That he hadn't even been a cop then. She'd heard about him being literally attacked by Rick Debenshire at Midnight's funeral; she'd even seen it on TV, because cameras had still been rolling. She knew that he hadn't let on then that he was actually working against Devereaux's people. He'd done undercover work without ever having had training, or even being recognized for it.

Another interesting piece of information she'd garnered about Mr. Collins was the fact that he'd interrupted a wedding in progress to remove the bride. Dave had told her about that. He had indicated that Christian and Susan had dated after that, but that Christian seemed to be back to playing the field again, much to the dismay of Susan's uncle, Rick Debenshire.

Then there was the colorful past that he supposedly had. There was scuttlebutt about murder and drugs. But while no one seemed to know much about it, it added another layer of mystery to the man.

Face it, O'Neil, you're hooked. The thought caused her to sigh out loud.

"Problems?" Christian asked, raising a jet black eyebrow at her as he pulled into the parking lot at the Computer Warehouse.

"Not a thing," Stevie replied automatically.

They got out of the car and went inside. Christian dealt with the salesman with authority and confidence, even chiding the man for trying to sell him "some cheap knock-off."

"I've got doorstops," Christian said, giving the man a wry look. "I don't need to pay 2K for another one."

The man immediately changed tactics, and they were done in fifteen minutes and headed to the business office to pay. The young woman who helped them seemed unable to keep her eyes off him. She kept stumbling over her words, stammering frequently, especially when he stared directly into her eyes with his baby blues. By the time they'd walked out of the office, Christian had managed to finagle extra memory, a second battery pack, and a carrying case for the notebook computer, all for free.

"You look pretty pleased with yourself," Stevie observed as they got back into his car.

Christian shrugged. "I save money where I can. Midnight needs all she can get."

Stevie nodded, a knowing look on her face. "Plus you can't resist exercising that lethal charm."

"Am I charming?" he queried, his eyes on hers.

"I'm sure you have your moments," Stevie countered as she smiled brilliantly.

"Ah," Christian said, grinning as he started the car. But before he could back out, a police car pulled up behind them. "What the—?" he started to say, noting it was a San Diego PD vehicle.

Stevie glanced behind them. "Oh crap." She rolled her eyes, shaking her head.

"Problem?" Christian asked.

"Constant." Stevie reached for the door handle just as a man walked up to the passenger side. She stood in the open doorway, talking to him. Christian couldn't help but overhear the conversation.

"What're you doing here?" the uniformed officer asked, sounding suspicious.

"Working," Stevie answered simply.

"In a Viper?"

"It's not mine."

"I know that, but who…" the man began as he leaned down to look across the car at Christian.

Christian stared back at him calmly. He didn't recognize the officer, but he could see he was Italian in descent and looked pretty brawny. It was apparent the guy knew Stevie, however.

"Oh," the officer said when he saw Christian.

He then took Stevie's arm and led her back to his car. Christian sat and waited, not able to hear the conversation any further. After a few minutes, Stevie came back, and the police car drove away.

"Fixed?" Christian asked.

"He keeps it up and he will be," Stevie replied mildly, but her eyes were narrowed.

Christian laughed at that, and started back to the office.

The first night they actually worked their case they did so sitting in Christian's room at Joe's house. Stevie looked over the room, thinking that Christian Collins had to make enough money from the department to afford an apartment of his own, considering he drove a $75,000 car. In all actuality, the "room" was an in-laws' quarters at the edge of Joe's property. Christian had never taken the time to look for an apartment. At least this way he was easily available when Joe needed him to watch out for his family. Joe still refused to let Christian pay him for the room, reminding Christian every time that he

77

was "family."

The small cottage was nicely furnished, and reminded Stevie of a studio apartment. The furnishings were all heavier wood pieces in dark tones, reflecting the man himself. The colors were deep navy blue and black or gray. Stevie realized it was very much fitting of what she knew, or thought she knew, about Christian Collins.

Christian leaned against the doorjamb, watching her look over his place. He realized she was probably wondering why he didn't have his own apartment or house, and found himself explaining.

"Never have taken the time to get my own place. This has always just been easier," he said, all the while wondering what it was about this woman that made him incapable of keeping his mouth shut.

Stevie nodded. "Where should I set up?" she asked, holding up the notebook they'd purchased earlier that day.

Christian pointed to the oak table set up near the kitchenette. She set down the notebook. Christian immediately set to work connecting the appropriate cables and phone lines. He gestured for her to have a seat, and she sat across the table from where he worked. Again she found herself watching everything he did. She noted he was wearing jeans, like he often did at work, but his beige cotton shirt was untucked and he wore no shoes or socks. This was a much more casual version of the Christian than she was used to.

Within ten minutes he had everything set up. He then had her sit in the chair in front of the computer and showed her how to log in to the chat community they were targeting. They came up with a nickname for her, Feisty16, and proceeded to make up a profile. Stevie Krenshaw was a sixteen-year-old sophomore at San Diego High School. Her interests included new adventures, talking on the phone, exciting chats, and fast cars. "Something has to be true," Stevie put in as Christian typed in the information, grinning at her.

The rest of the evening was spent getting into the chat room and letting her get the feel of it and familiarizing herself with the terms used. Christian sat next to her, answering any questions. He also pointed out the nicknames of some of the users he suspected of being adult men targeting young women. The chat room was a busy one, frequented by many teenagers in San Diego.

Two hours into the chat, there was finally something to pique their interest.

"Now what about guys like that?" Stevie asked, pointing to a user who had just asked about "young girls" in the room.

Christian watched the dialogue scroll for a few minutes, then nodded. "Try it, probably won't be that easy though."

"I could get lucky, though, right?" Stevie asked, glancing over at him.

Christian was leaning back in his chair, his arms crossed over his chest, his light blue eyes scanning the computer screen constantly.

"Just take it slow. I never trust the out-and-out ballers," he said, pointing to a line of text where BigMan_on_Campus was asking who in the room was sixteen.

Stevie went ahead and answered him. An instant message popped up from BigMan_on_Campus: Hi, looking for some fun?

Stevie typed in: Maybe.

BigMan_on_Campus: What will it take to make you sure?

Stevie looked back at Christian. "Ask him his age," he said.

Stevie typed in: How old are you?

BigMan_on_Campus replied: I'm 28.

"Usually means he's about forty," Christian said, grinning.

Stevie typed in: Are you married?

No, I'm single. Do you have a boyfriend?

Again Stevie glanced at Christian. He just looked back at her, knowing she needed to get the feel of this for herself. He wouldn't always be there to tell her what to say.

Stevie turned back to the screen, then typed in: I have one, but he doesn't really have the 411 on the important stuff, ya know?

BigMan_on_Campus jumped at the bait: He's not good sexually?

Stevie narrowed her eyes at the screen as she typed: He's a boy, this shorty needs a man.

Christian was impressed; she knew a lot of the terms the teenagers used, and he could see that she was capable of catching on to what needed to be done.

Stevie spent the rest of the evening chatting with Big-Man_on_Campus, getting his email address and an alleged picture of him. "Probably a fake," Christian said, since the picture was almost too perfect, the man too handsome, like it had been cut out of a magazine. BigMan_on_Campus wanted to know if he could call her. Stevie told him that her mom and dad didn't want her giving out her phone number. She told him that if he wanted to give her his number, she'd call him when she could. BigMan_on_Campus wasn't very bright, and gave her his number at work. He then told her his name was Mark.

She disconnected for the night and looked over at Christian. "Well?"

Christian nodded. "You did good…"

"But it isn't that easy, right?" Stevie put in, knowing that was what he was thinking.

"Well, you need to keep your options open. After a few nights, I'll log in from my computer, and we'll have to give them a bit of a show, so we'll get the worms out of the woodwork."

"Show?"

"Yeah," he said, grinning sardonically. "Something to get them interested."

Stevie gave him a pointed look. "Cyber? In the public room?"

Christian laughed; she did know the terminology. "Don't worry, we'll just give them a taste to get them going. No point in sitting in there night after night hoping someone will do what BMOC did, right?"

"True," Stevie agreed, having gotten really tired of watching some of the teens in the room as their chat became more and more stupid and inane.

"So, what part do you play in this?" Stevie asked as she stood and stretched.

"Well, I'm the technical end, for one thing, running down the ISP addresses."

"ISP what?"

"Addresses—it's basically the address for the computer they're on. It will, hopefully, give us a physical on the suspect."

"Hopefully?"

"Well, sometimes these guys know ways around the ISP thing,

but I know tricks too."

"Okay, so you're the geek on the case," Stevie said, grinning as his lips pursed in a scowl and he narrowed his eyes.

"I'm also the one that's gonna wipe that grin off your face if you're not careful," he said, looking directly into her eyes, his light blue eyes glittering devilishly.

"Oh-ho, tough guy, huh?" Stevie countered, putting her hands on her hips. "Gonna hit me?" she asked, grinning still.

"Not what I was thinkin'," he said smoothly, the look in his eyes changing subtly.

"Oh," Stevie said, her green eyes widening ever so slightly as she pointedly closed her mouth, pressing her lips together.

Christian broke into a smile, shaking his head at her. "Go home, I'll see you tomorrow."

"Okay, hacker sir," Stevie said, grinning again.

"There ya go," Christian said, grinning too.

Stevie left, leaving her notebook at Christian's since they needed to work together for the first few runs.

That night Christian lay in bed thinking about the exchange. He liked that she didn't respond to him the way he was used to women doing. He sensed that she was interested, but wasn't altogether sure why she wasn't doing anything about it. His first thought was that she was serious about Dave Dibbins, and she was being faithful to him. She wouldn't be the first woman to be faithful to a man who was rarely if ever monogamous. Christian wondered too about the officer who had basically dragged her away that day, probably to tell her he was nothing but trouble. Not that that wasn't true.

Christian liked doing what he wanted, with whom he wanted and when. Stevie O'Neil was a challenge, and he figured that was about it. She was fiery, and that attracted him. He'd heard a lot of people saying that she was basically a young version of Midnight Chevalier. That thought appealed to him too. Midnight was the one woman he wanted that he could never have. A younger version just might satisfy that appetite.

Then there was Susan. They hadn't even seen each other in the last month. He'd been purposely cool to her lately. There were times when the guilt of what he was doing would get to him, so he'd distance himself from her to give them some space. Usually, somewhere along the way, he'd pull her back to him again. He knew it wasn't right to act the way he did with her, but he couldn't seem to help himself. He craved more than she could always give. It annoyed him that he couldn't just break it off totally with Susan. The fact of the matter was, she was the safe haven he ran to when he needed comfort and someone familiar. The problem was, she wasn't the kind of woman that could handle such casual use. He wasn't sure what he was going to do about that one.

***

Rhiannon and Kyle needed to visit the warehouse where much of the department's surplus equipment was kept. Rhiannon offered to drive; Kyle accepted. She led him out to her classic Mustang.

"What year is this?" Kyle asked as they left the parking lot.

"Sixty-seven and a half."

"Wow, a real classic," Kyle said, smiling. "I have a fifty-six back in New York."

Rhiannon was still for a moment. "A fifty-six what?" she asked quietly.

"Chevy," Kyle said, looking over at her. He noticed her stillness, and subsequently her surprise.

She turned to look at him, her mouth slightly agape. "You have a fifty-six Chevy?"

"Yes..." Kyle said, giving her a bemused look.

"What color?" she asked, something important apparently hinging on his answer.

"Black," Kyle answered, his brows furrowed, wondering why she was acting like this.

Rhiannon nodded slowly. "Does it have flames?" she asked hollowly.

Kyle hesitated this time. It was apparent to him that she was very haunted, and he wasn't sure he liked the chilly feeling climbing up his spine. "It doesn't yet, but I was considering putting some on when I finish restoring it. Why?"

Rhiannon shook her head slowly, as if denying what he'd just said, then grinned to herself. Finally she came out of her trance-like state.

"Jason had a fifty-six Chevy, black with blue-black flames." She pinned him with a more direct look. "He restored it himself."

Kyle didn't speak for a moment, his mouth dropping open at the almost eerie coincidence. Finally he shrugged. "More than one man in the world with taste," he explained simply.

Rhiannon laughed. "Yes, that would have to be it."

They were both silent for a few minutes. Kyle broke it first.

"So how did you and Jason meet?" he asked.

Rhiannon's face took on a faraway look as she smiled. She looked over at Kyle. "He was my FTO."

"Really now?" Kyle said, smiling widely, appreciating how difficult that must have been for the two of them.

"How did you meet Barbara?" she asked, figuring it was safe to since he'd asked her.

"Well," he said, smiling again, "she was the cousin of one of my collars. I met her during the trial."

"She was related to your crook?"

"Yeah."

"That must have been fun," Rhiannon said, knowing it must have been anything but.

"Worse still," Kyle said, feeling strangely open with her, "most of her family was connected."

Rhiannon's mouth dropped open. "Mob?"

"Yep," Kyle replied, grinning lopsidedly.

"Good God! You win."

"In the who had more obstacles to overcome category?"

"Yes, sir," Rhiannon said, smiling.

Kyle chuckled. "Oh, cool."

They spent a few comfortable hours at the warehouse, going over what was stored where, and why. Rhiannon also showed him how she thought she'd approach inventorying the equipment. Kyle made a few suggestions and they discussed the merits of each. Rhiannon found that she liked Kyle's management style a lot. He listened attentively when she explained things, asked pertinent questions, and never presumed to tell her how to do her job. He made careful, considered suggestions, and never seemed to take umbrage if she didn't think his idea was a great one. Kyle also encouraged her to express ideas of her own. Oddly enough, she was finding herself comparing Kyle to Jason a lot, especially after the discussion that morning about the car.

While externally Kyle Masterson appeared to be worlds apart from Jason Templeton, with his well-dressed, highly groomed appearance, his expensive education, and his high rank in the department, when it came right down to it, Kyle was a nice, easygoing guy who also just happened to have an excellent education and a lot of power in the department. It was obvious that he didn't consider himself or his position above any other. He was more than willing to get down into the dirtiest boxes in the warehouse to get a feel for what was contained there, but would be just as comfortable in the office of any high-ranking official in the city. It was an interesting combination.

"So, if we want to, can we print the report with the cost of each item?" he asked, still attempting to come to an answer on how to prioritize the inventory search.

"Yes, we can, but…" Rhiannon trailed off hesitantly.

"But what?" Kyle asked, wanting to get her take on this whole process.

Rhiannon shrugged, leaning back against the desk. "The thing is, if you tell them how much some of this stuff costs up front, it'll make them more likely to claim they found the more expensive stuff, even though they didn't. Simply because they don't want to have to answer to the chief for losing expensive pieces of equipment."

"Don't they sign something saying they found this equipment?"

"Well, yes, they do." Rhiannon made a gesture of futility. "But let's face it, when a lieutenant or a captain is going to get their butt chewed, and they think they can avoid it, they might take that option."

Kyle nodded. "I see what you're saying," he said, looking a bit defeated. "So how do we ever know if we found everything?"

"That's the problem, sir."

Kyle sighed deeply, nodding. His eyes narrowed as he turned the problem over in his mind. He knew that Midnight wanted to have a clean inventory, and that she needed to make sure that nothing like what Devereaux had done ever occurred again. Devereaux had been diverting departmental property, especially guns and cars, to his drug-dealing friends. It had created a huge discrepancy between what they thought they had and what they actually had, and Midnight wanted it cleaned up and maintained with an audit trail from there on out.

"What says that the units do their own inventory? Is that a requirement?" Kyle asked, an idea starting to form in his head.

"It's just always been done that way before," Rhiannon said, grimacing. She hated sounding like what she considered to be a sheep. Doing things the way they'd "always been done before" wasn't something she was given to, but there were too many things to change all at once.

Kyle grinned at the face she made. "So it could be changed?"

"It could, but to what?"

"Create a team to handle the entire department's physical inventory. Train them on the specifics of what they need to do and how to do it," Kyle said. "That way, there's less likelihood of mistakes in how the process is handled, as well as not getting skewed results due to butt-chewing avoidance."

Rhiannon looked surprised by the idea, but Kyle could see that she was mulling it over. He liked that she never dismissed any idea out of hand simply because she didn't like it or understand it right off. Rhiannon Templeton definitely had a quick mind; he could see why she'd been a good narc. She was able to look at an idea or a plan and quickly point out any flaws in the design or execution.

"Who would be on the team?" she asked. "What type of staff?"

"Well," Kyle said, grinning at the fact that she'd already seen one possible problem, "it couldn't be anyone that has any stake in the outcome, so no ranking officers. Maybe secretarial pool?"

"Handling law enforcement equipment?"

"You, Collins, and I would be part of the team too, to oversee any confidentiality issues," he replied. "Besides, the whole pool should have had background checks, right?"

She smiled. "Yes, but do you want a secretary handling an MP5 or a Benelli?"

"Okay, good point there," he said, grinning back at her. "But I maintain that there will be three certified peace officers on the team. We could handle the weapons checks."

Rhiannon nodded. "You're right, we could." She was hiding her surprise at the fact that he intended to actually physically help with the inventory too. "We'll need official permission to create a team like that."

Kyle smiled mischievously. "Leave that to me—I happen to know the chief."

Rhiannon laughed. "I've heard you have connections."

So the day proceeded. They laid out their plan, coming up with a list of issues they'd need to deal with before they brought the idea to Midnight. They drove back to the office to work up a team suggestion list. They spent hours doing so. Kyle once again ordered lunch for them, insisting on paying since Rhiannon had driven out to the warehouse. Rhiannon suspected that Chief Masterson had serious issues with women paying for his lunch, but she said nothing, only grinning to herself as he explained his excuses.

At the end of the day, Kyle stood up and stretched, reaching for his jacket hanging on the back of the chair he'd been sitting in.

"So, what're you up to tonight?" he asked conversationally.

"Not much, Chief. I'm pretty dull," Rhiannon said, using his title out of habit.

Kyle grimaced. "Rhiannon, please call me Kyle or Masterson—'Chief' still sounds wrong to me," he added, grinning.

"Okay," Rhiannon said, smiling at the correction.

"So, I was wondering," he began hesitantly, "would you want to go have a drink somewhere? I'm feeling too wound up to go home just yet."

Rhiannon looked back at him, surprised by the offer, but even more surprising to her was the fact that she didn't want to refuse. She told herself that this was her chance to pay for his drink, to pay him back for getting lunch. If she'd been totally honest with herself, she would have admitted that she also wanted a chance to get to see Kyle Masterson outside of the work setting. Her heart wouldn't readily admit that though.

After a long hesitation, which had Kyle rethinking the wisdom of asking her, Rhiannon said, "That sounds great."

In the end, they went to a bar and grill. They sat at a table in the corner. It was nice and quiet back there. Kyle ordered a JD and Coke with an extra shot of Jack Daniels on the side. Rhiannon ordered a Baileys and coffee.

"This is a nice place," Kyle said, looking around. Rhiannon had picked it.

"I know," Rhiannon said, smiling. "My dad used to come here all the time—he used to bring us sometimes too. It's a good traditional Irish pub."

Kyle grinned. "Ah, that explains it. Was your dad a traditional Irishman?"

"He had his moments. He definitely had the Irishman's temper. Whenever Stevie would get herself into trouble, he could raise the roof with his voice alone."

"Did Stevie get into trouble a lot?" Kyle asked, raising an eyebrow.

"Enough, more after Dad died, though," Rhiannon said, a shadow crossing her features as she thought about it.

"He was killed in the line of duty, wasn't he?" Kyle asked softly.

"Yes, he was shot while on patrol," Rhiannon said, her voice softening too.

"I'm sorry." Kyle shook his head. "No one should have to lose two people they love so dearly to this job."

Rhiannon nodded, accepting his thanks and his words.

"Is that why you became a cop?" Kyle asked. "Because of your father?"

"Yes, that's why," Rhiannon said. "I mean, I always knew I wanted to do something pertaining to law, but I thought more along the lines of a lawyer. But when Dad was killed, it was like something inside me said I needed to take his place."

"And Stevie?"

"Stevie always wanted to be a cop. She always wanted to be Midnight Chevalier when she grew up."

"Seriously?" Kyle asked, grinning at the odd comment.

"Oh, yeah," Rhiannon said, nodding emphatically. "She met Midnight and Joe Sinclair the first time at our dad's funeral. But she'd heard about Midnight from our dad for years. He thought Midnight was the best example of a female role model in law enforcement. He actually said that. So when Stevie met her at the funeral, the impression Midnight made was tenfold. Both Midnight and Joe were like idols to her. When other kids had posters of rock stars on their walls, Stevie had the recruitment poster for San Diego PD and one of the FORS patches my dad had managed to finagle for her. I'm surprised she didn't get into a gang, just so she could quit it and get into FORS."

Kyle laughed. *Score one more fan for Midnight Chevalier*, he thought. "I've known Midnight for a lot of years—she definitely makes an impression on people."

Rhiannon gave him a sidelong glance, not sure if she should

91

mention the scuttlebutt that she'd heard. Kyle caught the look.

"What?" he asked, already sure what she was thinking.

"I just…" she said, hesitating, then figured what the hell. "The rumor I heard that you and Midnight were a couple years ago."

Kyle inclined his head to indicate that she was right. "We were, but it was about fifteen years ago."

"I guessed that much," Rhiannon said, smiling. "I can't see her having an affair on Rick Debenshire no matter how good-looking you are." The moment she said it, she felt like clapping her hand over her mouth. Had she really said that? Her face must have showed her mortification, because when she got the nerve to look at him, Kyle was grinning.

"Too much alcohol, Sergeant?" he said, his eyes twinkling with humor.

Rhiannon pointedly looked at her glass, which was still half full of lukewarm coffee, since she'd been doing most of the talking. "Not yet," she said, picking up the glass and downing its contents. "I think I need to excuse myself for a minute," she continued, standing up. "I need to go extract my foot from my mouth."

Kyle laughed. "Should I order you another drink?"

"Definitely," Rhiannon said, grinning at him. She turned and walked away from the table.

Kyle found himself watching her go, then shook himself mentally. *Jesus, Masterson, you're becoming almost human.*

The waitress wandered over while Rhiannon was in the ladies' room, and Kyle ordered two more drinks. The waitress made a point of being extra nice to him, leaning over far enough to let him get a view of her ample cleavage. When she brought the drinks back to the table, a feat that was managed in record time, before Rhiannon could get back, she "accidentally" dropped a stack of napkins. She bent far over to pick them up, once again giving Kyle a view of her assets. She stood, turning to wink at him, then went back to the bar.

Kyle glanced up to see Rhiannon moving toward the table. She had a sly grin on her face; she'd seen what the waitress had done.

"Enjoy the show?" she couldn't resist asking.

Kyle shrugged. "When I was alive, I might have found her interesting," he said with a straight face. The slow grin started a second later.

Rhiannon laughed, having gotten over her embarrassment from before. What did it matter if she thought he was handsome? He'd probably heard that from millions of women. It wasn't like it wasn't glaringly obvious.

"So, what about you, Chief Masterson," she asked, having realized she'd been doing most of the talking. "Why did you become a cop?"

"Seemed like a logical step after the SEALs," he said, shrugging.

"You were a Navy SEAL?"

"Yes, ma'am," he replied, inclining his head.

"Impressive."

Kyle shrugged, looking unimpressed with himself.

"How long were you in the SEALs?"

"Four years."

"Why'd you leave?"

"I just felt like it was time. I got the training I wanted—it was what I needed at the time. And I was ready to move forward with my life."

Rhiannon studied him for a moment. "What you needed at the time. What was that?"

Kyle grinned, seeing the investigator coming out of Ms. Templeton. "I needed some discipline. I had a bad habit of moving from one thing to the next when I got bored. I needed to learn to stick to one thing and perfect it before moving on. The SEALs taught me that."

"Then you went to college?"

"Yes, then I started college, and got into law enforcement a few years later."

"Wow, that's a lot."

"Didn't seem like it then. I was just a kid, and had boundless energy and no one to be responsible for but me."

"Do you have children?" Rhiannon asked.

"Yes, two boys," he said proudly.

"How old?"

"Brenden is five, Nicholas is thirteen."

"Wow, big difference," she said, smiling.

Kyle grinned. "Yes, Bren was our surprise. What about you—did you and Jason have kids?"

Rhiannon shook her head sadly. "The ironic thing is, the night before he died was when we finally talked about having kids."

"Damn..." Kyle said, wincing. "I'm sorry, Rhian," he said,

sounding genuinely so.

She nodded, feeling emotions well up in her throat. She took a few quick swallows of her drink to stave them off.

They spent a bit longer talking about other things, but it was getting late and Kyle needed to pick his younger son up from daycare. He drove her back to her car at the department. Once back in the parking lot, she turned to him.

"Thank you for this," she said sincerely. "This is the first time I've been out socially since Jason died."

"Same here," Kyle said, surprising her. "I'd like to take you to dinner sometime soon—would that be okay?"

"I'd like that," Rhiannon said, smiling at him almost shyly. She couldn't believe she was actually making a date!

"Great, we can talk about when. It's not like we don't see each other every day right now, right?" he said, grinning.

Rhiannon laughed. "True." It occurred to her then that she was making a date with her boss, much like she had with Jason. The co-incidences were stacking up. Maybe there was something to this. "I guess I'll see you tomorrow," she said hesitantly.

Kyle touched her cheek gently, and leaned down to kiss her lips very softly. When their lips parted, Rhiannon looked up at him, her emerald green eyes staring up into his. Kyle could read trepidation in them. He gave her a small smile, pulling her into his arms gently and holding her for a long moment, knowing that she was afraid of the same thing he was. Moving forward with their lives meant leaving behind the memories of the people they had loved so much and lost. It was a terrifying thought, but it was also a sign of life for both of them, and that was a welcome feeling after so many years of feeling dead inside.

***

Joe Sinclair sat on his bed staring off into space, an almost-empty bottle of tequila firmly in his hand. He was waiting for his wife to come home from school. He'd managed to hold it together to help put the kids to bed, then had grabbed the full bottle of Herradura and headed for his and Randy's bedroom.

Randy came in a little over half an hour later. She knew instantly something was wrong. Joe was sitting on the bed, fully clothed, his holster and badge still on as well. He was holding a now-empty tequila bottle. She walked over to him, her eyes already showing fear.

"What happened?" she asked.

"Randy," Joe said, his English accent thicker than normal because of the alcohol. "Sit down."

"Joe..."

"I had an appointment with the department doctor today. Just the usual yearly fitness evaluation," he said, staring straight ahead, as if reading off a script. "He noticed the cough that I can't seem to get rid of, so he checked it out. You know, thinking the usual pneumonia setting in..." He trailed off as he closed his eyes for a moment. When he opened them again he looked at Randy, and she could see fear in them, something she hadn't seen there very often. "Randy, he found a spot on one of my lungs." The words fell in the room like a death sentence.

Randy drew in a sharp breath, tears springing to her eyes.

"No, God, no," she whispered, shaking her head as if to deny what he'd just said.

She reached out to him, and he pulled her into his arms, hugging her to him. She held on to him for a long time. When she pulled back she looked up at him; his light blue eyes were fixed firmly on hers. She touched his cheek, and he closed his eyes.

"Okay," she said after a few minutes, her voice stronger now. "What is he going to do?"

Joe opened his eyes again. He could see the determined set of her jaw; she was rallying her strength to keep from falling apart. He took a deep breath, expelling it slowly to calm his own nerves.

"He said we need to do some tests, and they want to do a biopsy."

"Okay…" Randy said, her mind working already. "The biopsy is the only way they can determine what it is. He obviously doesn't think this is simply pneumonia, but that doesn't automatically mean it's cancer, Joe."

Joe nodded slowly, swallowing convulsively. For once in his life, he was facing something he couldn't fight with a gun or his fists, and it terrified him.

"So when does he want to start the tests?" Randy asked, smoothing her hands over his chest, trying to sooth away the tension she could feel in him.

"He said I need to make an appointment. He doesn't do that stuff, but he gave me a name…" He reached into his shirt pocket and pulled out a neatly folded piece of paper.

Randy took it and nodded. "Okay, I'll call first thing in the morning." She stood up and moved around to the other side of the bed, standing next to where he sat. She reached down and pulled his boots off. Joe sat back, just watching her. The alcohol was finally catching up to him, making him feel numb. Randy proceeded to undo his belt and take off his badge and holster, setting both up in their closet.

"Now," she said, facing him, her hands on her hips. "What have you had to eat tonight?"

Joe gave her a "You've got to be kidding" look.

"Okay, that answers that," Randy said, grinning at her husband. "I'll be right back." She left the room and Joe stared off into space. He couldn't believe after being in law enforcement for almost twenty years, after being shot God knew how many times, something like cancer could kill him. It was unreal.

Minutes later, Randy walked back into the room with a sandwich and a bottle of water. Joe groaned.

"Don't start with me, Sinclair. You've got to do something to counter that tequila or you'll be hungover as hell tomorrow," Randy said, sitting down next to him on the bed and handing him the plate.

Joe ate dutifully, almost automatically. After a while he started to feel less numb. Surprisingly, he was feeling more calm because Randy was calm. If she wasn't freaked out about this, why was he? Maybe it wasn't cancer. He'd managed to spend most of the afternoon convincing himself it was, but it could be a lot of other things, right?

Randy handed him the bottle of water halfway through the sandwich and told him to drink it all. "The water will help dilute the alcohol in your system."

Joe looked petulant, but drank anyway, knowing she was right.

When he finished, she took the plate and the empty bottle to the kitchen. She came back into the bedroom, kicked off her shoes, and sat next to her husband. Randy lay against his chest, and Joe's arm went around her to hold her to him. Her arm went around his waist as she snuggled against him. She kissed his neck, moving to his ear. "I love you," she whispered. "We'll get through this, and everything will be fine."

Joe felt tears sting the back of his eyes, and he turned to kiss her on the forehead. He held her for a long time, feeling her head pressed against the hollow of his shoulder. He didn't know that inside she was reeling with the thought that the man she loved could possibly have lung cancer. She knew at this point she needed to be brave and get him through this. Letting him stress himself out about it ahead of time would serve no purpose. If it turned out that he did have cancer, they'd deal with that then.

Randy knew, from past experience with Joe, that if she remained calm, it would help him do the same. She still remembered back when they'd first got engaged, when during a confrontation with some gang members one of them had grabbed her and held a knife to her throat, threatening to kill her if Joe didn't drop his gun. Joe had his weapon pointed at the man, but the guy was holding Randy in front of him like a shield. Randy had been confident in Joe's abilities as a marksman, and for that reason had been perfectly calm. Her calm and her communication of her confidence in Joe had in turn calmed Joe to the point of ice. Joe had known beyond a shadow of a doubt that he could drop the man if he even flinched like he was going to hurt Randy. It had saved Randy's life that night, and Randy intended to do everything she could to save Joe's life now.

Stevie and Christian were asked to come into the office by Kyle. Rhiannon and Kyle were in the meeting as well as Midnight. Rhiannon laid out the plan for the physical inventory, explaining that three other non-sworn staff members were going to be designated by Midnight and Kyle to work on the project as well.

After the meeting, Christian took Stevie down to his office to show her the inventory system so she'd better understand what they were doing. They were sitting in his area of the office when Tony walked in, obviously looking for Stevie.

***

Anthony Marconi was the classic badass Italian cop. He secretly thought he could be another DeNiro. He was decent-looking, and he could bust heads with the best of them. He'd been a patrol cop for seven years. He was all-time pissed off that he hadn't made sergeant yet. He'd taken the test twice, ranking low on the list each time. He knew, though, that as other guys got promoted he moved up on the list. In fact, before the test had been given again a year and a half ago, he was rank two; he could have been promoted. But he never was. He naturally blamed that fact on Midnight Chevalier. She was a broad, so of course she wasn't going to promote a lot of men, unless she'd screwed them first. Look at all her friends that were ranking officers. Now she had hired an Assistant Chief from across the country just because she'd screwed him years ago. The whole department knew it. Bitch!

And on top of that, the broad he'd been dating a year and a half ago had been made a sergeant too. Fuck! She'd only been with the department a little over a year before she quit. She hadn't taken any test. What she'd done was gone out and fucked her way into the cartel. What was this shit? She kills some guy in his own apartment, stitching him up and leaving the bloody mess. And what happens? She gets brought back into the department and promoted! Another bitch! But one he craved like no other woman he'd ever slept with. They'd had something good going before she'd left the department. She was a spirited little witch, and he'd been working on bringing her to heel, but then she'd disappeared.

Tony wanted her back now, just to show her that no matter what shield she wore, she was still only a broad and she wasn't so hot. He intended to bring her to heel and make her beg. When she was hooked on him again, he'd dump her ass. Now she was hanging out with Christian Collins. Another favorite of Midnight Chevalier's. Someone else that got a free pass to walk when he killed a cop. Tony knew he needed to get her away from Collins; the dude was bad news. Tony couldn't admit even to himself that Christian Collins was more competition than he could handle. He'd heard from one of his friends that she was in the building today and in Collins' company.

"Hey," he said, walking into Christian's area.

Christian and Stevie looked up from the computer. Christian, who sat on her left, so slightly behind her from where Tony stood, started grinning sardonically. Stevie gave an exasperated sigh.

"What's up, Tony?" she asked.

"Hey," he said, smiling at her, using his charm. "You haven't called me—I was getting all offended and shit."

Stevie's expression didn't change. "Look, Tony," she said irritably, "I'll call you when I want to call you. Okay?"

"Come on, Stevie, don't front me." Tony's eyes flicked over to Collins to see how he was enjoying this scene.

"I'm not fronting you," Stevie said, leaning back in her chair and looking up at him coolly. "I'm telling you that I'll call you when I damned well want to."

"Damn girl," Tony said, drawing it out, his voice what Stevie termed "all ghetto." "Why you gotta be like that?" His eyes flicked to Collins again. "Or are you passin' it out now?"

Stevie's mouth dropped open, but before she could speak, Christian sat up. He leaned around her, his arm coming to rest on the desk slightly to the front and to the side of Stevie, basically putting it around her.

"Yeah, she is," he said, his tone cocksure. "You got a problem with that?"

Tony's face suffused with color as he attempted to hang on to his temper. His eyes narrowed at Stevie as he refused to look at Collins' grinning face.

"You cunt," he said, then turned and walked out of the office.

Stevie was shocked, and stared after him for a long minute. He'd always been a bit of blowhard, but she couldn't believe he'd actually called her that. *Jesus! What an asshole*, she thought. She turned to look at Christian.

"We're sleeping together?" she asked, grinning.

Christian shrugged. "It got rid of him, right?"

"True."

"Alright then," he said, grinning back.

"Alright then," she echoed.

They went back to work and didn't think a thing about it again.

Later that afternoon, Stevie was in the stairwell, headed to her car. She heard her name called; she stopped, looking up the stairwell. Three men were descending from the floor she'd just come from. She warily recognized three of Tony's friends. She immediately stepped back to the corner of the stairwell, putting her back to the wall so she could keep an eye on them all.

"So, O'Neil," said one of the men, John Standish, looking her over with his brown eyes. "How's it going? Heard you were back."

Stevie nodded. She knew why they were there.

"You got nothing to say, O'Neil?" Bill Harris said, his bug eyes narrowing at her.

"She's too good for us guys," Tom Hill sneered. "She's a sergeant now."

"Yeah, I heard that," Standish said, his eyes chilling even more.

"Me too," Harris echoed.

"I'm not a sergeant, boys," Stevie said wearily. "Get your story straight. I'm actually doing sergeants' work and getting patrol officer pay."

"Yeah, that's not all we hear you're getting," Harris said. "We hear you're sleeping your way up."

Stevie gave them a condescending look, then said, "Well, I guess it's just too bad for all three of you that you're only patrol then, huh?" Her tone was smooth, but her anger was evident.

Harris moved toward her, pressing her back against the wall, as the other guys chuckled derisively. "Oh, you'll give it to anyone, O'Neil, we already know that," he said, pressing his body closer to hers. He was easily twice her size, and so were the other two men.

Stevie's head came up, her eyes blazing. "Back off, Harris. I mean it."

He didn't back off. In fact, one of the guys egged him on, saying, "Give it to her, Harris."

"What are you gonna do, Sergeant?" Harris said, his mouth down by her lips. His breath smelled of coffee and cigarettes. She could feel his hands sliding up her sides. She tensed with the intension of shoving him again, but he anticipated that and grabbed her wrists in a painful grip. "I don't think you're gonna do anything, bitch," he spat at her. "You'll take it and you'll like it. Women like you always do."

Before Stevie could muster a response, an English-accented voice called out from above, "Remove your hands, or I'll remove them for you."

Stevie's head snapped up, as did Bill Harris' and his cohorts'. Christian stood midway down the stairs on the flight above them, leaning down with his light blue eyes narrowed.

"And what're you gonna do?" Harris said, obviously feeling pretty full of himself at that moment. "Gonna shoot me too, Collins? Think you can shoot us all?"

Christian descended a couple more stairs, his face taking on a calmly confident look. "I don't even have my gun out, Harris," he said smoothly. "But I will kick your ass."

"Yeah," said yet another voice from above. They all looked up and saw Spider Nguyen standing on the landing above them. "And when he's done kicking your asses, I'll put you all on report." He grinned maliciously. "That's after I get done helping him."

104

Bill Harris looked back at Stevie; she stared at him, her green eyes unblinking. He pointedly took his hands off her, holding them up and out to his side, stepping back and turning to face Spider. "Hey, Lieutenant, we were just messing with her. No harm intended."

Spider looked at Harris for a long moment before his eyes moved to the other two men, then to Stevie. She hadn't moved, her face showing no emotion, her chin still raised slightly in feigned confidence.

"In my office," Spider said, looking at Harris, then Standish and Hill. "Now."

"But, Lieutenant—" Harris started.

"Now," Spider ordered, his voice a low growl.

Harris glanced at Stevie again, leaning down to say, "This isn't over."

Stevie just gazed back at him, her face giving nothing away.

"Harris!" shouted Spider. "Do you *want* to be riding a desk for the next month? Or would you prefer to be busted down to meter maid?"

Harris turned and walked up the stairs, and the other two followed, giving Stevie a pointed look. When Harris walked by Christian, he said, "You wait."

"Bring it, anytime," Christian replied calmly, staring back at the other man. The three of them went up and out of the stairwell, and Spider stood looking down at Stevie.

"You okay, O'Neil?" he asked, his voice much more official than the look on his face. His eyes showed the sympathy he felt for her situation. He'd heard enough to know that no matter what, Stevie was

105

going to be treated like she'd done something underhanded and gotten rewarded for it.

Stevie stared up at him, nodding, her face still stone-like. "Thanks, Lieutenant."

"No problem," Spider said, then inclined his head toward Christian. Christian just nodded back, as if getting a message from Spider telepathically. Spider turned and walked through the door he'd come out of just a few minutes before. He'd been headed downstairs to take a break when he'd come upon the scene in the stairwell.

As he went through the door he almost bumped into Midnight, coming the other way. She'd been down at the FORS offices, letting Rick's crew know how he was doing. Rick was resting at home for the moment, but Midnight figured he wouldn't put up with that for long.

"Hey, Spider, what's up?" she asked, noticing the harassed look on his face.

Spider grimaced, shaking his head. "Some guys strong-arming Stevie O'Neil about her 'promotion.'"

Midnight's face became serious right away. "Strong-arming how?"

"Saying she slept with someone to get it, and that she should give them some too," Spider said, his tone of voice showing his distaste for the men's attitudes.

"Well," Midnight said lightly, although her green eyes were already showing sparks of anger, "last time I checked, I don't sleep with women. So there goes that theory. Where are they now?"

"In my office," Spider said, the beginnings of a grin on his face.

"Let's go." Midnight gestured for Spider to lead the way.

Spider walked into his office followed by Midnight, and the three men's faces literally turned white. Spider sat down at his desk, and Midnight went to perch on the credenza behind it. Her eyes moved from one man to the other, but she said nothing.

"Now," Spider said, leaning back in his chair, his eyes on Harris. "What was all that about?"

Harris didn't say anything at first; he didn't know what all Spider had heard. He shrugged. "Nothing, Lieutenant. We were just messing with her, like I said before."

Spider stared at the man for a long moment, his eyes boring into Harris'. "What were you *messing* with her about?"

"You know," Standish said, shrugging in an overly casual way. "The fact that she got so lucky to get promoted to sergeant."

"Lucky?" Spider echoed.

"Yeah," Harris said, nodding. "Lucky. Do you know how many of us have been on the sergeant list for years?"

"No, how many of you?" Spider replied, his eyes sparkling with restrained anger. He was beginning to wonder if one of these guys, or all three of them, were the ones who'd written the letter to the city council. He glanced back at Midnight and saw that she was thinking along the same lines; although her face gave nothing away, her eyes connected with Spider's and he just knew.

"A lot of us, man," Hill said, sounding exasperated. He was sweating profusely. He'd never had to face Spider Nguyen, let alone the chief. He was the type that usually flew low under the radar, did as little as possible, and stayed out of everyone's notice. He knew that what they had just done was stupid; he could just kick Tony's ass for putting him up to it.

"Well," Spider said, leaning forward and steepling his fingers in front of him, "that's a damn shame." His eyes pinned Harris. "So where did 'You'll take it and you'll like it' fit into this good-natured messing with her thing?"

Harris paled slightly; he'd hoped that Spider hadn't heard that part. He glanced at Midnight and noted the green fire that was now being turned directly on him. "Sir, I was just joking around. You know that old sleep-your-way-to-the-top thing. It was just a joke."

"Did that joke involve manhandling Stevie O'Neil too?" Spider asked.

"I didn't manhandle her, sir," Harris said defensively and with almost the right degree of self-righteousness.

"I think the bruises that she'll likely have on her wrists will prove a lot differently, Harris."

"Sir, I—"

"I've heard enough," Midnight said, standing. "Harris, you're on report, and you've got three days on the beach. Get out of here."

Bill Harris sat looking at her, his mouth open in shock. "Three days for this?" he said derogatorily.

"This, Harris? This?" Midnight repeated incredulously. "You think you can push women around in this department? You think, for that matter, that you can push anyone around in this department just because they got the promotion you think you deserved? What you did is called sexual harassment—ask your union rep to explain it to you." Her arms were down at her sides, her fingers working like they did when she was readying for a fight. "Let me tell you something, Officer Harris. You're still with this department only because it's too much work to fire your ass. I've seen your jacket—you make more mistakes and cause more liability issues than any officer on your beat. Don't think for a minute that I don't know what goes on in this department, and believe me, if I don't, someone I know does." Her eyes moved to the other two men. "And you two, follow the leader ended in grade school. Next time follow someone with more sense, and a better attitude about the women in this department. It'll get you much farther." She glanced at Spider, who was sitting back in his chair, enjoying the show. "Spider, I'd like to see an incident report on this in my office today by five—can you handle that for me?"

"You got it, Chief."

Midnight nodded. "I'll meet with Stevie O'Neil and see if she wants to press assault charges on Harris here." She pinned the three men with another long, hard look, then walked out.

Meanwhile, in the stairwell, Christian descended the steps. He walked over to Stevie. "You okay?"

Stevie's eyes were closed, and she was taking slow, deep breaths as she nodded. Christian reached out, touching her on the shoulder. He could feel that she was trembling, and was fairly sure she was desperately trying to hold it together. It hit him hard that she was so shaken; he wasn't used to seeing her vulnerable at all. He had to clamp down on the urge to take her in his arms; at this point he figured she might slug him, just to vent some of her tension.

Christian leaned against the wall beside her, pulling out a cigarette and lighting it. He waited for her to get her composure back. After a few minutes she did, leaning against the wall and bumping her shoulder against his arm.

"You're not supposed to do that in here," she said, gesturing to

109

the cigarette.

Christian grinned. "And?"

Stevie was silent for a long moment. "Thanks for that," she said finally. Christian merely inclined his head to her. "It isn't over though, you know," she added.

He nodded. "I know."

"I don't think you should get yourself any more involved—Tony's crew can be pretty nasty if they want to be." Stevie shrugged. "Besides, it's me he's pissed at, not really you."

"Well, I'm already involved," Christian pointed out. "I involved myself when I claimed to be sleeping with you." He looked highly unconcerned.

"Yeah, but—"

"Shut up, O'Neil."

Stevie stared back at him for a long moment, then grinned. "You got that gallant streak from your cousin, huh?" She'd heard all the department's stories about Joe's chivalrous acts.

"Nah," Christian countered. He grinned. "I just like to stir shit up."

"Uh-huh," Stevie said, sounding unconvinced.

"I think from here on out, though, I'll walk you to your car," he said, dropping his cigarette and stepping on it to snub it out.

"Think that'll put them off?" Stevie queried as they started down the stairs together.

"You're right," Christian said, grinning slyly. "I'll need to move in with you."

Stevie laughed, feeling better again. Maybe having a guy like this around wasn't so bad after all. Even if he was a serious temptation.

***

Dave Dibbins lay in his bed at home, staring up at the ceiling and attempting to breath very carefully. His back felt like it was on fire. He took slow, deep breaths, concentrating on relaxing the muscles in his back. Nothing was working. The intercom above his head buzzed. He reached up and depressed the button, wincing as the movement sent all new spasms down his back.

"Yeah?" he gasped.

"David?" queried a familiar female voice with an English accent.

"Susan?" he said, surprised. "What are you doing here?"

"Rescue mission," Susan said, smiling.

"Come on in." Dave pressed the button to unlock the door.

A minute later, Susan walked into the room, looking delicately pretty in her cream-and-pink dress, her hair pulled back from her face in a loose braid.

"I heard you were in an accident," Susan said, concerned, as she looked him over. "Are you alright?"

"I'm still in one piece," Dave said, grinning at her.

Susan canted her head to the side. "I see that, yes," she said, sounding very English.

Dave chuckled. "So, to what do I owe this unexpected pleasure?"

Susan smiled at the sweet comment; Dave always had a way of

putting things that made everything sound like a compliment.

"Well, my aunt asked me if I could come over here and make sure you were fed and watered properly."

Dave laughed, then winced as the action hurt his back.

"What hurts?" Susan asked, immediately concerned.

"My back," Dave said, grimacing. "I jacked it up pretty good."

"And just how did you manage to do that?"

"I rolled a car," he said casually.

Susan gasped. "Not yours?"

"No, no," Dave said, shaking his head. "If I'd rolled the Charger I'd be a lot more depressed than this." He grinned. "Fortunately for me, and unfortunately for Midnight, I rolled a department car. The Charger is too well known in some of the areas I work."

"How did it happen?" she asked, sitting carefully on the bed, mindful not to move it at all as she did.

"Bad guy ran, I chased, bad guy had a buddy that rammed me from the side, I went off the road and rolled it in a ditch."

Susan shook her head even as she smiled at his simplified version of events. He definitely wasn't one given to drama.

"Okay, did they give you something for the pain?"

"They did."

"And you took it when?" she asked, smiling down at him.

"Uh," he said, looking chagrined, "I haven't."

"And why, pray tell, is that, Mr. Dibbins?"

"'Cause I can't take it yet."

"And why is that?" she asked in mock exasperation.

"I haven't eaten yet."

"Oh," she said, looking embarrassed at not realizing that. "I guess I could do something about that."

"Susan, I didn't mean…" Dave said, trailing off as she shook her head.

"Just lie there and I'll be right back," she said, and left the room.

Dave grinned, thinking she certainly was bossy when she was in charge of someone.

A few minutes later she came back with a sandwich and a glass of milk. He started to sit up, groaning.

"Don't sit up," she ordered, sitting down on the bed and placing the milk on the nightstand.

Dave looked at the milk, then back at her. "I haven't drunk milk since… well, I never drank milk."

"Well, you will now. It will coat your stomach better, so the medicine doesn't upset it."

"Are you always this bossy with your charges?" he asked, smiling up at her.

"Careful," she cautioned, "or I'll make it a point to short-sheet your bed."

"You wouldn't dare," he said indignantly.

"I would so," Susan said, laughing lightly.

Dave gingerly picked up a piece of the sandwich and ate it. Before the next bite, he asked, "So what's going on with you? Anything new?"

"Nothing really," she said as she watched him eat. "Very relieved my uncle is alright after that shooting."

"Yeah," Dave said, shaking his head in wonder. "Still can't believe he was brave enough to do that."

"It was incredibly gallant—almost insanely so, though," Susan agreed.

"Well, the way I understood it," Dave said, taking another bite of sandwich and even reaching over to drink a little milk, "he couldn't duck and cover because the kids were directly behind them, and he didn't want to chance either of them getting hit."

Susan nodded, having heard the story from Midnight.

"So what about you?" he asked, watching her closely. "Anything new with you specifically?"

Susan grinned, knowing he meant Christian. "Yes, as a matter of fact. I've decided to start dating other people."

"Good," Dave said. "Any prospects yet? I know they've probably been lining up in the hopes that you'd notice."

"Oh, stop it," Susan said, laughing softly. "There is certainly no line. But there is a young man at school that has been hinting around that he'd like to take me out."

Dave smiled. "There you go."

"I don't know, though," Susan said, sighing deeply. "I'm not sure that it's fair to date anyone right now."

"Fair?"

"Well, to whoever I date."

"How so?"

"Well, any relationship I have now will most likely be doomed."

"Oh, God, you aren't talking about all that transitional relationship nonsense are you?"

"It's not nonsense, David—really, it's not," Susan said. "I've been studying psychology, and basically a person needs to go through another relationship to get over the last one. But the one that comes after the bad one is merely a stepping stone, and therefore doomed."

Dave rolled his eyes. "Okay, whatever you say," he said, his tone still cynical. "Besides, who says you have to jump right into a relationship? Why can't you just date a few guys and play around a bit?"

"Play around?" Susan asked, giving him a caustic look. "After all I've dealt with, having Christian do that to me?"

Dave grinned. "Yeah, it'll be good for you."

Susan made a face. "I don't think I could do that anyway. I'm just not a casual relationship kind of person. It's all or nothing for me."

It was Dave's turn to sigh. "Just promise me one thing."

"What's that?"

"That you'll at least date a couple of guys before you jump back into something heavy." He held up his hands as she started to shake her head. "I didn't mean at the same time. But don't settle for some mediocre guy just because he asks you out, okay?"

"You mean, avoid the Warren situation this time?" she asked, smiling.

"Exactly."

Warren was the man she'd been engaged to marry when she met Christian. Christian had knocked her socks off; with his incredible good looks, sensual ways, and bad-boy nature, she was thrown completely for a loop. He'd allowed her to see a side of him almost no one had ever seen, and it had made her fall completely and hopelessly in love with him. Warren had none of Christian's qualities, and had quickly paled by comparison. The fact of the matter was, she was marrying him because her family thought he was suitable, and Susan hadn't known any better than to admit, even to herself, that she really didn't love Warren. It had taken Christian walking in during her wedding and telling her that he loved her to get her to give up the insane idea of marrying a man she didn't love. Even if she didn't end up with Christian, he had saved her. She knew she would have ended up like her own mother, in an unhappy marriage for many years because she didn't have the drive to get out of it.

"I promise you, I won't settle for anyone but Mr. Right," Susan said, holding up her right hand.

"That's what I want to hear."

Stevie walked in then. "Dave!" she said, moving to the other side of the bed—she looked scared. "Are you okay?"

"Stevie, I'm fine," Dave assured her.

"When I heard you rolled…"

"I know, babe, I know," Dave said. "That's why I left you a message to tell you I was fine." He knew she was thinking about how her brother-in-law had been killed.

Stevie leaned down, kissing him on the lips. She touched the cut on his cheek and the bruise on his jaw. "You're sure you're okay?"

"I'm sure, really. I just jacked my back up a little bit."

Stevie straightened up, nodding, and then looked at Susan questioningly.

"Oh, you two probably never met," Dave said. "Stevie O'Neil, this is Susan Endicott. Susan is here taking care of me during my invalid status."

Susan stood and extended her hand to Stevie. "It's nice to meet you. You're working with Christian, aren't you?" she asked, making sure to keep her tone light.

"Yes, I am," Stevie said, taking Susan's hand. "He's a good guy."

Dave snickered, drawing both women's eyes to him. "What?" he said, doing his best to look innocent.

"You know very well what, David Dibbins," Susan said.

Dave grinned.

"Okay, what part did I miss?" Stevie asked, looking between them.

"We were just discussing how Susan needs to see other people and stop waiting for Mr. Collins," Dave said matter-of-factly.

Stevie looked at Susan; she knew she was the woman Christian was dating. She also knew that Christian did pretty much whatever he wanted, including sleeping with whoever he wanted.

"Susan," Stevie said, her tone serious, "never wait for any man. None of them are worth that."

"Hey now!" Dave said with mock indignation.

Stevie shrugged. "Face it, Dave—It's a fact."

Dave gave her a sour look. "No, it's not a fact. You just have to find the one worth waiting for."

"If I have to wait for him, he's not worth it."

Dave just shook his head. "Women!"

"Men!" Stevie said, grinning down at him.

Susan watched them, amused by the whole thing.

Dave glanced at his clock, then back at Stevie. "Aren't you supposed to be working tonight?"

"Yeah," Stevie said, checking her watch. "I just wanted to stop by and make sure with my own eyes that you're alright."

"I'm fine, go do your thing."

"Okay," Stevie said. She leaned down and kissed him, then pulled back and touched the cut on his cheek again. "I'm glad you're okay. I don't know what I'd do if I lost you now, my friend."

"You won't lose me—I'll be around for a long time," Dave said, reaching up to brush her hair back from her forehead.

"Good," Stevie said. She stood up, looking at Susan. "It was nice to meet you. Take good care of this guy for me, will ya?"

Susan smiled. "I'll do my best."

After Stevie had left, Susan walked over to Dave's dresser, where the bottle of medicine sat. She read the dosage and took out one pill, then walked back over and handed it to him. He sighed, propping himself up on his elbow, wincing as he did, then took the pill with a swallow of milk, grimacing at the taste.

Susan smiled, thinking he was a lot like the children when they took their medicine.

"Is Stevie one of your girlfriends?" she asked mildly.

Dave shrugged. "She's someone I'm seeing, but she's just like me, playing everything fast and loose. We make good friends though."

"That's always good. I think even if Christian and I never end up back together, once everything calms down, we'll be good friends too."

They talked about other things then. They discussed the news article that had come out about Midnight. Dave told her about the group lynching they were planning for whoever had written the letter. He had her laughing almost to the point of tears as he told her about the conversations he and the other members had had that day.

After about an hour, it was obvious that the medicine wasn't helping that much. Whenever Dave moved wrong he'd wince, or let out a slight groan.

"You're still hurting, aren't you?" Susan asked softly.

Dave nodded. "Yeah, a lot."

"Okay, do you have a heating pad?"

"In the closet," he said, gesturing. "Top shelf, to the left."

Susan opened his closet, surprised to find that it was quite neat and orderly. The heating pad was exactly where he'd said. She plugged it in and carefully slid it under his back, while he showed her where it hurt. After about twenty minutes, she told him to turn over carefully onto his stomach.

"Why?" he asked, dreading the idea of trying to turn over.

"Because now that the muscles have been heated up, we need to smooth them out. It should help," she said softly.

"Okay," he said, and slowly turned over, gritting his teeth and allowing himself only one low moan once he got to his stomach. He put his arms up on either side of the pillow under his head.

Susan was trying to figure out how she was going to be able to massage his back at the angle she was at when she actually looked down at him. Fortunately, her small gasp came out right about the time he moaned, so he didn't hear. He'd had the sheet up over his chest the whole time she'd been there, so she'd only seen his arms bare, and even then she'd made a point not to look. He was a family friend, after all. But seeing his back bare, with all the sinewy muscles there, she realized that she'd never really seen Dave Dibbins without a shirt on. Since he was so slim, she'd always assumed he was skinny. Apparently, she'd been wrong. Very wrong. It surprised her that she found that she was attracted to him.

Shaking herself mentally, she slid her hands over his back, feeling for the bunched-up muscles that were causing him pain. She heard him let out a low moan and saw his eyes close; it sent a shiver through her. Forcing herself to concentrate, she found a knot in his muscles. Working gently, she loosened it. She felt him flinch.

"Does that hurt?" she asked, her hands stilling.

"Just a little," he said, his voice muffled because his mouth was half against the pillow.

"I'm sorry," she said sincerely.

"It's okay."

She saw his arms flex, and figured he was probably clenching his fists. She made a point of being even more gentle. She noticed the tattoo on his arm then.

"I didn't know you had a tattoo," she said, surprised that she hadn't noticed it before.

Dave glanced down at it. "Yeah, from my gang days."

"That's right, you were in a gang too," Susan said, just remembering that now.

"Yeah, started out in FORS with your aunt and Joe."

Susan shook her head. "Sometimes it's so hard to picture any of you as gang members. You all seem like such good, kind people. The idea of gang members conjures up images of drive-by shootings and drugs."

"Well, we did that stuff too."

"You did?" Susan said, stunned.

"The drug part, anyway. My gang was a distributer for a pretty big dealer."

"Really?" Susan asked, fascinated in spite of herself.

"Oh yeah. I made the deal with the source, and my gang did the selling on the street."

"My lord, that must have been dangerous."

"Not near as dangerous as having Joe Sinclair rat you out to your own members," Dave said, grinning.

"He what?" Susan said, her voice rising in her shock.

Dave smiled at her indignation on his part. "I was skimming from the profits—I figured it was my deal, so I should get half. My gang didn't need to know that part, they just needed to take what I gave them, as far as I was concerned. Anyway, Joe decided that the best way to get rid of me and my drug-selling gang was to inform my members that I was skimming."

"What happened?"

"Oh, they just about killed me."

"Oh my God," Susan said. "What was the purpose in that?"

"Well, a gang is a lot like a snake—if you cut off the head, the rest of it dies. Joe knew that, so he put it in motion."

"It could have gotten you killed!"

Dave laughed at her apparent upset. "Hey, it's okay. It was Joe and Spider that saved my ass in the end too. Oops, sorry," he said, realizing he'd cussed in front of her.

"Not to worry," Susan said, waving away his apology. "I've heard much worse around my uncle and Joe. So what did they do?"

"Well, they found me and hauled me into an old abandoned building. Then they told my gang where to find me."

"They did not!" Susan said, aghast once again.

Dave grinned, knowing he was getting Joe into trouble. "Don't worry, Susan, it was also Joe and Spider that protected me from my gang."

"So what happened?"

"I ended up standing with them to fend off my own people, and decided after that to join FORS."

"If you can't beat them, join them?" Susan asked, grinning.

"Exactly."

Susan shook her head, looking down at the tattoo again.

In the end, she had him turn on his side, and lay down on the bed behind him, where she continued to massage his muscles until he fell asleep. She thought about all that he'd told her. It was interesting, hearing all this about how he came to be a police officer. The odd thing was, she knew all the people he was talking about, but she'd never known everything about them. It was like sitting with a relative and learning things about your parents or a distant cousin. Suddenly you had a new insight into them. She listened to Dave breathing, and before she knew it, had drifted off to sleep herself.

She woke early the next morning, and realizing she still had her shoes on, she kicked them off, flexing her toes. When she opened her eyes, it was just breaking dawn outside, and she saw that sometime during the night, Dave had turned over and was now facing her. He was still asleep. She looked at him for a few long moments. She noticed the cross he always wore; reaching out, she touched it, feeling its texture. It was very detailed, and she lifted it to see it better. Her fingers brushed Dave's skin, and he opened his eyes almost immediately.

"Oh, David, I'm sorry," Susan said, aghast. "I didn't mean to wake you."

Dave grinned tiredly. "It's okay, I usually get up about this time anyway."

"You do?" she asked, glancing at the clock behind him. "At five a.m.?"

"Yeah," he said, moving carefully to lie on his back. "I usually go surfing first thing in the morning."

"Every morning?"

"Just about," he said, staring up at the ceiling.

"Doesn't that scare you? Being out there all alone?"

Dave grinned, glancing over at her. "Susan, I hang out with gun-toting drug dealers with really bad manners every day. Not much scares me anymore."

Susan shook her head in amazement. "I don't know how you do it."

"Do what? Surf or face drug dealers with manners issues?"

"Stop it," she said, smiling at him. "I mean facing people who might want to kill you."

"Life's too short to worry about how and when I'm going to die," he said, shrugging and wincing from the action.

"Hurting again?" she asked, touching his shoulder.

"Yeah."

"I'll go fix you something to eat so you can take some medicine," she said, and carefully got off the bed.

"Okay, thanks," he said, smiling up at her.

Susan left the room. When she came back a little while later, she stopped in the doorway, watching him. He had moved himself to the side of the bed and was sitting very straight-backed, with his feet planted on the floor. His eyes were closed, his hands down on his thighs. He wore only sweatpants, so his chest was bare, and she found that it was just as nice as his back had been the night before. It was well muscled, but not in a bulky way; he had a very lean, strong build. He was also very tanned. Again she found herself attracted to him.

As she watched, he took a slow, deep breath, his chest expanding, then blew the breath out slowly through his parted lips. She smelled the scent of incense and looked around, spotting incense smoke emanating from a bottle on his dresser. Captured by the scene, she stood holding the plate and glass, leaning against the doorjamb. It was obvious he was concentrating on what he was doing; he didn't seem to have noticed her at all. At least, she didn't think so, but after a couple of minutes, he turned his head in her direction and opened his eyes.

"You don't have to wait—it's okay," he said calmly.

"What were you doing?" she asked, curious now, feeling like she'd interrupted a ritual.

"Basically," he said, moving to sit back, "I was meditating to get some control over this pain."

"You meditate?" she asked, ever surprised by this man.

"Regularly," he said, smiling. He went on to explain as she handed him the toast and orange juice. "When I was shot last time, the medication they were giving me wasn't helping, and I kept getting sick from it. Spider taught me a lot about holistic medicine then. He taught me about centering myself, calming exercises, and about healing myself through the power of my mind and body." He shrugged, grinning. "I don't believe all of it, but some of it really helps."

"Wow," Susan found herself saying. She shook her head. "You are certainly an enigma, Mr. Dibbins."

"Why do you say that?" he asked, having heard the same thing from Stevie a few weeks before.

Susan shrugged. "You're just nothing like I thought you were. I don't mean that in a bad way," she rushed to add when he started grinning. "I just mean that I've known you all this time, but I've apparently never really known you at all."

"Question is," he said jokingly, "do you like what you're learning?"

"Very much," she said softly.

125

Dave's blue eyes widened slightly at her reply, but he said nothing.

CHAPTER 4

Stevie awoke to the sound of knocking on her bedroom door.

"Come in," she said sleepily, thinking it was Rhiannon.

"Stevie, it's me," said a now-familiar English-accented voice as the door opened slowly.

"Christian?" Stevie glanced over at the clock; it was 11:30 p.m. "What the hell are you doing here?" She turned on the lamp.

"I told you I was coming over to check your connection. You were having problems staying connected, and that won't help our case much," he said, a jet black eyebrow lifted at her sardonically as he noted her lack of attire.

Stevie glanced down, pulling the sheet up higher. Fortunately nothing had been showing, except her shoulders and a decent amount of cleavage. "You told me you were coming over tonight?"

"Yeah, I did." He grinned. "Maybe you were too busy flirting."

"Ugh," she said, rolling her eyes. "Don't remind me of all those sickos on there."

"Where's your notebook?"

She pointed to the desk by the window. Christian went over and turned the notebook around, checking the cables before turning it on. "Everything looks good here," he muttered more to himself than to her, then turned the notebook on. Stevie turned over on her side, propping herself up on her elbow to watch him work. She grinned to herself; anyone else would have been uncomfortable with the fact that their co-worker was lying there naked behind them. Not Christian Collins—he treated it like any other night. *Probably seen so many naked female bodies in his lifetime they don't impress him anymore.*

"Saw your girlfriend tonight," she said casually.

"You saw Susan? Where?" he asked with mild curiosity, glancing over his shoulder.

"She was at Dave's place when I went to see how he was," Stevie said, watching him closely to see how he reacted.

He made a "huh" sound in his throat. "Wonder what she was doing there. Midnight probably asked her to help out." He didn't sound the least bit concerned.

"That doesn't bother you at all?" she asked, not able to help herself.

Christian turned to her, puzzlement clear on his face. "Why should it bother me?"

Stevie turned onto her back, looking up at the ceiling. "Oh, I dunno... Dave's a pretty good-looking guy..." She glanced back at him pointedly.

Christian laughed and shook his head. "She wouldn't go for Dave."

"You don't think so?"

Christian gave her a look. "Just because he's attractive to you, doesn't mean he will be to her. You and she are totally different typewise."

Stevie nodded, looking unconvinced. "So what if she did? Went for him, I mean. Would that bug you?"

Christian turned back to the computer. After a few moments he shrugged. "I have no idea. It's never happened."

"She's never gone for another guy while's she's been with you?"

"Nope," he said, still tapping away on the keys.

"I don't get it." Stevie sat up, tugging the sheet up to keep herself covered as she pulled her knees to her chest and wrapped her arms around them.

"What don't you get?" he asked, glancing back at her again.

"Do you love her?"

He hesitated for a minute then nodded. "Yeah, I love her."

"So why can't you manage to be faithful to her?" she asked, almost sure he was going to ask her why she thought it was her business.

He surprised her by shrugging again. "I don't know. I need something more than she gives me."

"What's that?" she asked, really curious now.

Christian turned to look at her again, vexation darkening his features. "I don't know—I really don't. I guess I get bored."

"You get bored with her?" Stevie asked, no accusation in her voice. He nodded. Stevie could tell he felt lousy about it too. "Have you tried it?" she asked. "I mean, tried to be with just her and no one else?"

"Yeah, I tried it—for six months I wasn't with anyone but her."

"And what happened?"

He shook his head. "It didn't work. I wanted out—I felt like I was in a cage. I was craving more."

"But what? What do you crave?" Stevie asked, really wanting to understand him.

"Excitement," he said. "And passion, and… hell, even some drama now and again." He sat back in the chair, looking unhappy suddenly. "Susan would be more than happy to get married, have babies, and stay home to take care of them." He shook his head. "That's just not for me. I need someone that challenges me constantly."

"But you said you love her," Stevie said, still mystified.

"Yeah… I don't understand it myself."

Stevie thought about it for a minute, then said, "Well, you love her, but you're not *in* love with her."

"What's the difference?"

"Well, you can love someone, care about them deeply, worry about them, want the best for them, but it doesn't mean you want to be with them all the time." She shrugged. "To me, being in love with someone means you want to be around them all the time—you can't think of anyone you'd rather spend time with. You miss them when they're gone, you just can't wait to see them again. I guess you crave them."

Christian looked thoughtful for a minute, then nodded slowly. "Maybe you're right. I don't know. I know I really hate who I am when I hurt her feelings."

"But you can't be with her, and that hurts her feelings, right?"

"Yeah," he said, looking miserable.

"You love her," Stevie confirmed. "She's just not the one you're meant to be with."

Christian looked at her for a long moment, surprised that she'd said that. But he couldn't deny it; he'd suspected it for some time now, but he'd never really admitted it to himself. He'd always told himself and Susan that if he ever got married, it would be to her. He'd been settled with that thought, but now he saw that it wasn't really true anymore. He couldn't see himself married to Susan; he'd be a cheating husband within a year. He wouldn't do that to himself or to her.

He sighed as he turned back to the computer.

"So it's my turn," he said, glancing back again.

"Your turn to what?" Stevie asked.

"To ask questions."

"Okay," she said, taking a dramatic deep breath. "Shoot."

"You still seeing Dave?"

"You mean am I still sleeping with him?"

Christian laughed at her directness. "Yeah."

"I haven't been the last couple of weeks."

"But that doesn't mean you aren't anymore, does it?" Christian asked, already knowing the answer.

"Nope."

"Sleeping with anyone else?"

Stevie leaned back against the headboard, getting comfortable. "Not at the moment, no."

"What was the deal with Tony?"

"Jesus, you ask a lot of questions," she said, rolling her eyes.

"Didn't you just ask me a lot?"

"Yeah, I guess I did."

"Alright then," he said, and waited.

Stevie shook her head, then grinned. "Okay. Tony was a guy that I dated back before I left the department. He's this blustery big mouth that was under the impression he was going to tame me."

"Oh he thought so, huh?" Christian said, grinning. He could only imagine how a woman like Stevie would take that.

"Oh yeah," Stevie said, rolling her eyes. "He thought he was being slick about it, but he's pretty dumb—it was easy to tell. He was even trying to get me to move in with him. Like that was ever going to happen." She shrugged. "As it turned out, leaving the department at least got me away from him."

"But now…"

"Now he thinks because I'm back, that means we're a couple again."

"That's why he pulled you away from the car that day, isn't it?"

"Oh yeah, he wanted to know what the fuck I thought I was doing with a player like you. I tried to explain to him that I was working with you, but he just got all pissy at me. So I told him I'd call him to get him out of my face."

Christian laughed. "That's why he was pissed that you hadn't called him."

"Yep," Stevie confirmed.

"Tough," Christian said seriously. "And who were those guys earlier today?"

"Friends of his from the academy. They're sheep." Her tone showed her distaste for the men.

"Think he had anything to do with their getting up in your face today?"

Stevie thought about it, then nodded. "Probably did."

"Then I'd say he needs to be taught a lesson."

"No, Collins," Stevie said, making a cutting gesture with her hand. "I don't want you any more involved than you already are, okay? These guys are stupid, but they'll fight to protect their own."

Christian looked back at her for a long moment, then turned back to what he was doing on the computer. A couple of minutes later, he said, "Got it. I had to reset some stuff, but you should be okay now." He turned around in the chair.

"Why did it get messed up?"

He shrugged. "Sometimes these things get squirrely and just reset themselves."

"Great," Stevie said, rolling her eyes. "Should you maybe show me what you did, so I can fix it next time?"

Christian raised a jet black eyebrow. "You wearin' anything under that sheet?"

"Uh, no."

"Then I think you'd better not get out of that bed," he said, his tone holding an undercurrent she couldn't put her finger on.

"No? Why not?" she asked, challenging him.

"Because if you do, a lot more than your computer is going to get taken care of."

Stevie laughed, then nodded, looking appropriately solemn. "I understand."

"Do you?" he asked, staring back at her with his light blue eyes.

"I think so," she replied, nodding wisely.

"And what is it you think?"

She shrugged casually. "Just more than you can handle, is all."

Christian's mouth dropped open in surprise. Then she could see the ego kick in as his eyes narrowed. Slowly, he stood from the chair, all six feet two inches of him. Stevie couldn't help but admire the picture he made. He wore black jeans, black leather boots and belt, and a denim work shirt. There was no denying the man was insanely handsome.

As she stared back at him, refusing to look away, he walked over to the bed. He put a booted foot up on the sideboard, looking directly into her eyes, not breaking the stare as he reached out and pulled the sheet out of her hands. He stripped it down and off her totally, and only then did his eyes drop to her body. His lips parted. He dropped the sheet and slid his hand behind her head. Stevie was mesmerized by his actions, unable to even form a complete thought beyond *Oh my God!*

In one fluid motion, Christian leaned down and pulled her forward, his lips covering hers hungrily. The moment their lips connected, there may as well have been an explosion. The heat that went through both of them was undeniable. Christian groaned against her, even as she moved to kneel in front of him on the bed, her lips never breaking the connection, her hands sliding up his chest to his shoulders. His hands were at her back instantly, dragging her body against his. His kiss increased in passion, his tongue sliding between her lips, demanding entry.

It was Stevie's turn to groan as his tongue licked at her lips hungrily, sliding between them, meeting hers and moving over it. Her moan had him dragging her off the bed, holding her against him, her feet a full five inches off the floor. Turning to the wall, he pushed her against it and pressed his body against hers. His hands went to the wall on either side of her head for a moment as she encircled his waist with her legs.

She pulled his shirttails out of his pants, attempted to undo his buttons, kissing him all the while. He pushed her hands away as he leaned back slightly, pulling the shirt off over his head and tossing it aside. His hands went back to the wall as hers eagerly explored the muscles in his back, reveling in the smooth hardness of his skin. Pulling her lips from his, she moved down his neck, kissing his skin, her nails leaving light marks down his back as she dragged them down it. He groaned loudly, dropping his head back. He felt her teeth on his skin a moment later and was sure he was going to explode. His hands went to her body, caressing, exploring, making her writhe.

Her legs dropped from his waist as she dropped to her feet. She moved her hands to his belt, pulling at it, loosening it. Christian watched her as she unfastened his jeans, pulling them down along with his underwear. His hands went to her waist immediately, lifting her and pushing her against the wall again, pressing against her as he brought her down his body with expert care. Stevie's hands grasped his shoulders as his body entered hers, her legs once again wrapping around his waist. No sooner was his body inside her than she was gasping in her first orgasm, her nails leaving deep marks on his shoulders, his lips at her neck, his teeth nipping at her skin.

Christian had to fight to control himself, but he was determined to take his time. He'd been craving her for too long; he knew that.

Once Stevie's initial lust was sated, she was determined to get to him. Her lips moved down his neck, biting and sucking at his skin. His hands moved into her hair, guiding her. She slid her hands over his back and down his chest, her fingers caressing his skin, touching his nipples.

"Jesus…" he whispered hoarsely, knowing what she was doing and feeling more of his control slip away. His hand moved to her hair, entwining itself in it, using a handful of its silky length to pull her head up and guide it back to his lips. His lips took hungry possession of hers again, starting yet another fire in her body. She groaned, biting at his lower lip in protest, even as her body responded strongly to his aggression.

"I want you to—" she began, but his lips stopped her. She shook her head, trying to pull back. "Damn it, Collins," she growled. "I want you to—"

"I will," he interrupted, his voice a growl too. "Come with me."

The words themselves sent her over the edge again. They both cried out in their release, her clutching at his chest, his hands at her waist, pressing her down on him harder. They both gasped for breath, trying to gain control of their heartbeats again. Christian dropped his head to her shoulder. She rested her head against his, sliding her hands up around his neck.

After a few minutes, Christian slipped one arm around behind her, grasping her waist, and steadied them with his other hand as he moved away from the wall. He held her to him as he sat on her bed, her legs still around his waist. He kicked his boots off and reached down, pulling the rest of his clothing off. Stevie's hands were already in his hair again, clutching at him. In leaning forward to remove his pants, he had put his lips against her shoulder; he kissed it now, nipping at it too. Stevie's hands clutched at his head, pulling his face up to hers so she could kiss him. Within minutes they were kissing passionately again. Stevie pushed him back on the bed, moving her body over his. They made love again, and afterward lay across her bed, trying to catch their breath. Christian shifted to lie the right way on the bed, pulling her with him. Stevie moved to his side, her hands still running over his body.

"You have a body that does not quit, Collins," she said reverently.

Christian grinned. "I could say the same for yours, O'Neil."

They lay in silence for a while, still trying to still their heartbeats.

"So," Christian said, still slightly out of breath, "why'd you make me wait so long?"

"So long?" Stevie echoed incredulously. "Collins, we've only known each other a little over two weeks."

"Yeah," he said, pulling her closer, "but we've wanted each other since the second we met."

"We have?"

Christian looked down at her, his eyes searching hers. "You didn't want me?"

"Hell yes, I did. I didn't know if you wanted me."

"Like crazy," he replied seriously. "So why'd you give me an opening tonight?"

Stevie shrugged. "I figured, what the hell—if you said no I could just shoot you." She started grinning then, and he laughed. "So what's your story, Collins?" she asked, curious about him.

"What do you want to know?" he asked, settling comfortably on his back, his arm around her waist, pulling her in close to his side.

"I know you're from England and you're Joe Sinclair's cousin—that's about it."

"Well, I'm from London, born and raised there," he said, staring up at the ceiling. "My father is an English lord."

"Seriously?"

"Yeah," Christian said, not sounding too impressed. "My mother was a maid in his household." He looked at her to see how she reacted; she just nodded, waiting for him to continue. "Anyway, he fired her as soon as she told him she was pregnant. So she left, had me, and raised me on her own."

"Strong woman," Stevie said. "Must be where you get it from."

Christian grinned. "Must be."

"So where did you learn about computers?"

"I took some classes for a while, thinking I'd do that for a living. I seemed to have a knack for them, but…"

"But what?" she said when his voice trailed off.

Christian shrugged. "I needed more money than that would make me, and I needed it then."

"For what?" she asked, noting the look on his face; he was hesitant to tell her something.

"Well, I had to pay rent on two flats, so…"

"Why two?"

"Well, there was mine, and then there was my mother's."

"You paid for her place too? Why not just have her live with you?"

Christian looked down at her, one black eyebrow quirked. "Ever try getting a leg over when your mother is in the same house?"

Stevie laughed, nodding. "Actually, I did once when I was in high school—you're right."

He grinned. "High school, huh?"

"Oh yeah," she countered haughtily. "How old were you when you lost your virginity?"

"Thirteen."

"Thirteen!" she exclaimed. "Jesus, you were much worse than me. I was sixteen."

"Yeah, how old was he?"

"He was eighteen, and a senior and the school bad boy," she said, grinning.

"Oh," Christian said, nodding knowingly. "Always had a thing for bad boys, huh?"

"Oh yeah, can't stand them too pure," Stevie said, making a face. "Takes all the fun out of them if they're too wholesome."

Christian laughed, shaking his head.

"So what about you?" she countered again. "I mean, you are dating Susan—she seems awfully pure."

"That's what attracted me to her."

"Wanted to see if you could get to her, huh?" Stevie asked wisely.

Christian grinned; she did know his style already, didn't she? He nodded. "In the beginning, that's exactly what it was. She was this total wallflower in dowdy clothes, no makeup, her hair all up in this knot."

"Really?" Stevie asked, surprised. "She's beautiful—I can't see her being dowdy. She reminds me of one of those serene English debutantes."

Christian nodded. "Well, she is that. Her family has a lot of money back home."

"Ah, well that would explain her speech and manner."

"Yeah," Christian said, giving her a curious look. "This kind of stuff doesn't bug you at all, does it?" he asked, though it was more a statement than a question.

"Why should it bother me?" she asked, surprised.

"Well, we're lying here in bed, discussing my girlfriend…"

Stevie shrugged. "I don't see why that should bother me. I'm not looking to be your next ex-girlfriend or anything."

Christian grinned, shaking his head. She did have a way with words. "You are definitely different, Stevie O'Neil."

"I do try." She levered herself up on her elbow. "I was wrong, by the way."

"About what?" he asked, amused now.

"You can definitely handle it."

He grinned. "Sorta, huh?"

"Sorta a lot," she replied, leaning down to kiss his chest, moving her tongue over his skin to his nipple, nipping it with her teeth, hearing his sharp intake of breath in response. Minutes later they were making love again. Neither of them slept that night.

The following day they were both in Christian's area when Stevie got the message, via Spider, that Midnight wanted to see her. She looked at Christian, who just shrugged.

A few minutes later, Stevie knocked on Midnight's door. Midnight called for her to come in.

"You wanted to see me, Chief?" Stevie asked, glancing at Kyle Masterson, who had stood when she entered. She nodded respectfully to him.

"Yeah, Stevie, come on in," Midnight said, motioning for her to sit down.

Stevie closed the door behind her and sat down. Kyle took the seat next to her.

Midnight leaned back in her chair, putting a booted foot up on her lowest desk drawer. "I heard there was a confrontation between you and some of the guys yesterday."

Stevie was silent a moment, absorbing the fact that Midnight knew about the incident. "Yes, ma'am," she said hesitantly. "But it was nothing, just the usual hassle."

"I heard that Harris got physical," Midnight said casually.

Again Stevie paused. *Shit!* was all she could think.

"Well, ma'am," she said, making a point of keeping her hands down in her lap below Midnight's line of sight, because there were dark bruises where Harris had grabbed her. "He was just being a guy, you know?" She glanced at Kyle then, noting the "Oh really?" look he gave her. "Sorry, sir."

"Don't worry about it, O'Neil. I'm used to man-bashing—I work with Midnight." His grin was sly.

"Thanks," Midnight said sourly, giving him a dirty look.

"Glad I could help," Kyle countered smoothly.

Midnight looked back at Stevie again. "Look, Harris has been suspended for three days."

"Shit," Stevie said before she could stop herself.

"Stevie," Midnight said imploringly, "we can't put up with that kind of sexual harassment in this place. I can't," she qualified.

"Yeah, Chief," Stevie replied. "But you know the code."

"Yeah." Midnight nodded. "I know it, and you didn't rat anyone out. I ran into Spider after the incident and invited myself to his meeting with them. There's no way they can believe you caused Harris' suspension."

"Sure there is," Stevie replied, her green eyes sparkling with ire. "They can blame me for all of it. If I didn't screw someone to get promoted, then they wouldn't have had to hassle me about it and Harris wouldn't have gotten caught trying to rape a fellow cop and got his ass beached." Her anger at the situation was evident, and Midnight couldn't help but see herself in Stevie O'Neil at that moment.

She glanced at Kyle; he looked back at her as if asking, *What did you expect?*

"Look, Stevie, I'm sorry," Midnight said, shaking her head. "I lost it with Harris and beached him, and I can't undo it now. But I'm guessing it's pretty safe to say you don't want to press assault charges, right?"

"Sure I do," Stevie said acerbically. "And while I'm at it I'll just shoot myself with my own gun."

"Okay, okay," Midnight said, grinning and holding up her

hands in surrender. "I had to ask."

The intercom buzzed. Midnight pressed the button. "Yes?"

"Chief, Rhiannon Templeton is here to see Chief Masterson," said Cassandra.

"Okay, thanks, Cass. Send her in."

Stevie stood up, ready to leave.

"Stevie?" Midnight said.

"Yes, ma'am?"

"If anything else happens, I want to know about it, okay? If I'm not around, I want you to get ahold of Kyle or one of my people."

Stevie looked at Midnight for a long moment. She had the distinct feeling that Midnight didn't intend to handle any other incidents as officially. There was a knock on the door, and Midnight called, "Come," but never looked away from Stevie. "You got it, O'Neil?" she asked.

"Yes, ma'am." Stevie inclined her head. "Thank you."

She turned to leave and saw her sister standing in the doorway. "Hey, Rhi," she said, grinning at her.

"Hey, Stevie," Rhiannon said, smiling.

Rhiannon was still dealing mentally with the image she'd encountered early that morning. She'd walked in on Stevie and Christian, because she was so busy reporting that someone had been stupid enough to park a Viper outside their house. Fortunately for everyone involved, they'd only been talking at that point, and Christian had been covered from the waist down. Nonetheless, it still reddened her cheeks to think about it. Christian's comment in reply to her apology had been "I'm the stupid one," his grin in place as usual. The man

143

knew no shame!

"Good morning, Rhiannon," Kyle said, smiling warmly with the slightest hint of familiarity, just enough that Stevie caught it. She glanced at her sister to see her smile back at him. *What's going on there?* she wondered.

"Good morning, Chief," Rhiannon said, her smile almost shy.

Stevie left the office still wondering, making a mental note to ask her sister what was going on with the gorgeous Assistant Chief.

Back in Christian's office, she told him what the meeting had been about. He grinned when she told him what Midnight had said about getting ahold of her if something else happened and what she thought that meant.

"You're probably right," Christian said. "Midnight doesn't take lightly to people screwing with her friends. She's still into street justice."

"Yeah, but that's usually reserved for the Gang."

"The gang?"

"Yeah. You know, Sinclair, Debenshire, Nguyen, Dibbs, Ako, Sorbinno—all the old timers, and then of course you, Curtis, and Franco, the new kids."

"I didn't realize we were considered a gang," Christian said, amused by the term.

Stevie gave him curious look. "Where have you been, Collins? Everyone in the department knows about the Gang. You don't screw with one of them unless you want all of them down on your neck."

144

Christian grinned; that was true enough. "Okay," he accepted. "But I'd say that if she's protecting you now, you're part of the Gang too."

The idea gave Stevie a shock. She was part of the Gang; she was accepted by Midnight Chevalier. Wow—would wonders never cease. It was almost like achieving one's dream. Funnily enough, it seemed like high school, when you finally got accepted by the most popular kids. Only this was real life, and it meant a lot of respect and support she hadn't had for years. She wasn't sure if she deserved it or not. The people in the Gang weren't like kids in high school; they'd earned their reputations for their hard work and achievements at being the best at what they did. It just so happened that most of them started out in the department with or because of Midnight Chevalier. Stevie didn't feel like she'd earned their acceptance, not yet anyway, but it touched her that maybe she was accepted by them.

Joe went into the FORS offices on the first day that Rick came back. He walked straight to Rick's office, putting his head in and catching Rick on the phone. Joe waited, leaning against the doorjamb.

Rick hung up shortly thereafter. "What's up?" he said, looking at his best friend since childhood.

"Got time to come to Midnight's office with me?" Joe asked. His voice held a note that caught Rick's attention; something big was up, he could feel it.

"Yeah, no problem," Rick said, standing immediately.

Joe led the way as they headed to the elevators. They were knocking on Midnight's door a couple of minutes later. When they walked in, Kyle was sitting in front of Midnight's desk; he stood. Joe waved him back to his seat. "You need to stay for this too."

Rick walked over to stand behind Midnight's chair. Midnight looked worried; all Joe had said when he called to see if she was available was that he needed to talk to her. The fact that he'd brought Rick meant it was something she wasn't going to want to hear. She also didn't like the fact that Joe didn't sit down. He was pacing, which meant he was too restless, which meant he was nervous about something.

"What is it?" she asked, unable to stand the tension.

Joe stopped and looked at her, and then his eyes touched on Rick's. "I need to take a few days off." Midnight nodded, knowing there was more; Joe wouldn't go through all this for a couple of vacation days. "I'm checking into Mercy this afternoon."

"Jesus…" Rick breathed.

"Joe? What is it—why?" Midnight asked anxiously.

Joe hesitated, his light blue eyes closing for a moment. "The departmental doctor found a spot on my lung."

"Oh my God…" Midnight said, tears in her eyes instantly. Rick put his hands on her shoulders, and she reached up to take them. Neither of them saw the stricken look on Kyle's face.

Joe nodded at their reaction. "I check in this afternoon for all this shit they want to do."

Midnight nodded blindly.

"When will they do the biopsy?" Kyle asked, all too familiar with the process.

Joe looked at the other man. "Today at three."

Kyle nodded. "That's good—that's fast. The sooner you know,

the better." Joe nodded, looking pale. "Joe, it could be a lot of things—it doesn't have to be cancer."

"I know, I know," Joe said. "Randy's been telling me the same thing."

"How's Randy taking it?" Midnight asked.

"She's handling it pretty well—she's determined to get us through it. She's been making all the calls and setting the stuff up." He shook his head. "I don't know what I'd do without her right now."

"Well, you don't have to find out," Midnight said as she stood up. She walked over to Joe, and he took her in his arms. "It'll be okay, Joe," she whispered against his chest as he hugged her. "We'll be here with you through everything too."

Rick walked over, and while Joe still held Midnight, extended his hand to him. Joe clasped it, nodding. He looked like he was barely holding it together. Kyle watched the three of them, not doubting for a second that they'd get through this.

Twenty minutes later, Joe walked into Christian's area.

"Hey, man," Christian said, looking up from the computer he and Stevie were working in front of. "What's goin' on?" he asked, noting the look on Joe's face.

"Look, I need a favor," Joe said quietly.

"You got it," Christian said, standing up. Stevie sat back and watched them quietly, trying to be unobtrusive. "What do you need?" Christian asked.

"I need you to move up to the house for a few days."

"Okay…" Christian said, waiting for the rest; he assumed Joe was going out of town.

147

"I'm going into the hospital for a couple of days."

"Fuck man, what's going on?" Christian said, his stomach knotting instantly.

"I don't know yet. They found a spot on one of my lungs. I need to get it checked out." Christian said nothing, too stunned to even formulate a response. "Anyway, I need to know my family will be safe…" Joe trailed off as he thought about the fact that, if in the end he died, he'd need someone to take care of his family permanently. The idea made him feel physically ill.

Christian caught the connotation in Joe's statement, and swallowed a few times before saying, "You got it, man, no problem." His voice was gruff with the emotion he was suppressing.

"Thanks," Joe said, nodding. "I knew I could count on you. I'm checking in this afternoon. The kids get out of school at three—Susan will pick them up, but she's over helping out with Dave right now, so…"

"Don't worry about it, Joe. I'll take care of it. You just worry about yourself for a bit," Christian said, doing everything he could to keep himself calm and try to offer some kind of support to his cousin.

Again Joe nodded. "Well, I better get back upstairs. I have a ton of stuff I want to finish before I leave today."

Christian nodded.

Joe glanced at Stevie then, noting that there were tears in her eyes. He nodded to her, inexplicably touched by the fact that a virtual stranger was upset on his behalf. All he knew was that he wanted this over, and soon. He needed to know what to prepare for.

After Joe left, Christian sat down heavily in his chair. He looked like he was in shock.

"You okay?" Stevie asked, her own voice still emotional.

Christian looked at her for a long moment, as if he couldn't even think of anything to say. Finally he just shook his head. Stevie stood up, grabbing his hand and tugging him up too. She grabbed his jacket off the coat rack on the way out and pulled him outside to the motor pool. Christian just allowed himself to be led, then leaned against a wrecked squad car while she reached into his jacket pocket, pulling out his cigarettes and lighter. Taking one from the pack, Stevie lit it and handed it to him. Christian took a long draw. Stevie set his jacket aside on the hood of the car. Standing in front of him, she leaned in, laying her head against his chest. His arm went around her shoulders, holding her there as he smoked.

They stayed out in the parking lot for the next half hour, until Christian felt more in control again. When he moved off the car, Stevie stepped away, turning to go back inside. Christian grabbed her arm, pulling her back to him. She turned, looking up at him in askance. His hand came up, touching her face gently. Leaning down, he kissed her lips with more gentleness than she'd thought him capable of. When he pulled back, he looked down into her eyes.

"Thank you," he said simply. Stevie nodded, feeling warmed by his action. As they walked back inside, Christian put his arm around her shoulders, drawing her close. It was a gesture of possession, one Stevie would normally resent, but at that moment it felt good.

Kyle was sitting in his office, staring out the window at the bay. His mind was far away, remembering the day Barbara had come home to tell him she had breast cancer. She had been so calm, it had been almost impossible to believe what she was saying. He had gotten home early that day; it was almost Christmas and he wanted to make sure he had time to wrap her present. She'd chided him so often for her presents still being in whatever bag the store put them in when he'd bought them; that year was going to be different. He was still looking for the wrapping paper when he heard the apartment door open. He had to drop the box containing the diamond ring he'd bought her, the one she'd been eyeing for months, and push it under the bed with his foot.

When she walked into the room, he knew something was wrong, but he figured it was just another crisis with Nick; the boy was always in trouble.

"What happened this time?" Kyle said, grinning at his wife even as he admired her lovely figure in her blue jeans and T-shirt. He went to sit on the bed, and Barbara came around to stand in front of him. Her blue eyes searched his.

"Kyle, I need to tell you something," she said, her voice soft, as it almost always was.

"So tell me," Kyle said, still sure it was something about Nick.

"I have breast cancer," she said simply, just like that. No prelude, no beating around the bush. Barbara had always been like that; she made things simple when they could have been so complicated.

He stared at her for a full minute, trying to assimilate what she'd just told him. Breast cancer? That meant she'd have one or both breasts removed, right? Or chemotherapy? Or... *Oh my God!* He stood up, looking down at her, every emotion he was feeling churning in his bright green eyes. He was unable to get a word out; he felt so sick, and the lump in his throat kept threatening to come up. He reached out and pulled her into his arms, hugging her tight. He tugged her down on the bed with him and just lay there holding her. Barbara ended up holding him, caressing his back, telling him everything would be okay.

Nothing had ever been okay again, although Barbara did everything she could to minimize the impact of her illness on all of them. She'd gone on doing everything she'd always done, even when she was sick from the chemotherapy. When Kyle had begged her to take it easy, to slow down, she had told him simply that she wanted to enjoy the simple things in her life while she could. Kyle's career had ground to a halt—he was almost never at the department—but the chief understood; his own daughter had died of breast cancer years before. Kyle spent every moment he could with his wife and kids. No matter how much time he spent, no matter how many hours at night he lay holding his wife, awake in their bed while she slept, all he could think was, *It's not enough, I need more time.* But he didn't get more time.

She died in July of the following year. Just under seven months after she'd been diagnosed. The day of her funeral, he was putting on his tie tack. His hands were shaking so badly he'd dropped it on the floor. He gotten down on his hands and knees to get it because it had bounced under the bed. He found the diamond ring he'd dropped there months before. Nick had found him a half hour later, sitting on the floor of his bedroom, tears running down his cheeks as he held the ring he'd never given his wife. At the funeral he put it on her finger, kissing her cheek softly, whispering, "I love you," praying that she could hear him one last time from wherever she was now.

It had taken a month before he was ready to go back to work.

When he did return to the department, he threw himself into his job, working harder than he ever had in his entire life. He'd made Assistant Chief a year after his wife died. She had always told him he could be running the department if he wanted it bad enough.

There was a light knock on his door that interrupted his reverie.

Reaching up to wipe at the tears on his face, he said, "Enter," his voice hoarse from all that he'd been reliving.

Rhiannon stepped inside, closing the door behind her. Turning around, her eyes went directly to him sitting at his desk. She knew instantly that her instinct had been right. It was spreading like wildfire through the department that Joe Sinclair might have lung cancer and that he had announced it to the chief and Assistant Chief at 10 a.m. It was eleven o'clock now. When Rhiannon had heard, she had somehow known hearing about Joe's news would trigger all sorts of emotions in Kyle. She had debated with herself for a few minutes on the wisdom of going to see him, but in the end, she realized she would have done anything for someone to talk to many times after Jason had been killed.

"Kyle..." she said softly, her eyes saying everything her one word didn't.

He nodded, closing his eyes against the pain again. Rhiannon walked over to him and knelt down, taking his hands in hers and looking up at him. "Talk to me," she implored.

He did. He told her about the day Barbara had come home with her diagnosis. He told her everything he'd just been thinking about. In the end, Rhiannon was crying silently for him. When he finished his story, he came out of the trance he'd been in while telling it, having felt the need to distance himself from what he was saying, and saw Rhiannon's tears. She'd got up during his story, and now leaned against his desk facing him. Kyle stood and, smoothing his thumb over her cheek, wet with her own tears, smiled miserably.

"We certainly make a healthy pair, don't we?" he said.

Rhiannon laughed through her tears. "Yeah, real healthy."

Kyle smiled at her. He looked at his watch then. "So, can I take you to lunch?"

"Is that instead of dinner?" she countered softly, grinning.

"No," he said, touching her under the chin. "I still want to take you to dinner. But I need to get out of here for a little bit." He gestured around him. "And I think you could use a little bit of air too."

Rhiannon nodded, reaching up to wipe at her tears. Kyle handed her a handkerchief; she laughed lightly at that. "I didn't think men carried these anymore."

"My wife always bought me them," he said softly, then shrugged. "I figure I can still carry them—I'm old."

"You are not," she gasped, narrowing her emerald green eyes at him.

Kyle chuckled. "Am so."

He took her to lunch, and they talked about everything but the spouses they'd lost. It was an unspoken agreement that they'd relived enough pain at least for that day. They both returned to work feeling much more alive than they had that morning, and with a deeper appreciation for whatever God in the Heavens had brought them to help each other.

CHAPTER 5

Christian called Susan at Dave's house to tell her about Joe. Susan sat staring at the phone for a long time afterward. Dave, who had been taking a shower in an attempt to start moving around again, walked into the kitchen and saw the stricken look on her face.

"Susan?" he said quietly.

Susan turned to him. She had tears in her eyes. Dave went to her and took her in his arms. Her arms went around his waist as she buried her face against his bathrobe. He held her for a long time, not knowing what was going on but sure it wasn't a good thing. When she finally lifted her head to look up at him, he could see she was more in control of her emotions now.

"Christian called," she said softly. "Joe announced to my aunt and uncle that he may have cancer and that he's going into the hospital today for tests."

Dave stared at her dumbfounded. "Damn…" he finally said, shaking his head. He reached for the phone immediately and called Spider, Susan still standing in the circle of his arm.

"Spider, it's me," he said into the phone. He listened for a bit, then nodded. "I know, Susan just told me." Again he listened. "What time?" He glanced down at Susan and gave her a small smile. "We'll be there," he said then, and hung up a minute later. He looked at Susan again as he set the phone down. "Joe's biopsy is at three—we're all going to meet up at the hospital at five to see what's going on."

Susan nodded, then bit her lip. "What about the children? I'll need to go pick them up at school."

Dave narrowed his eyes in thought. "Okay, we can pick them up and see if Marie will take care of them while we go to the hospital."

Susan nodded. "I'll call her." Marie was Midnight and Rick's au pair, hired originally to take care of Mikeyla and staying on to help with Ricardo. "Should you be up this much?" she asked as she dialed her aunt's number at home.

"I'm gonna go lie back down right now," he said. "Let me know what Marie says."

"I will," she said as she watched him walk down the hall. She realized that suddenly she was being included at the vigil at the hospital. Three years before, she'd been home with the children when everyone else had been at the hospital for hours. It felt good to be included this time.

A little while later she walked into Dave's room; he was lying on his bed, staring up at the ceiling, apparently deep in thought.

"David?" she said softly.

His sky blue eyes flicked over to her. Without a word he held out his arm. Susan moved to lie carefully next to him, and his arm went around her shoulders comfortingly. She was careful not to put any weight on him, but he pulled her closer. She realized then that he needed comforting as much as she did.

Joseph Michael Sinclair was an icon to all of them. He was the pillar of strength when everything else around them went crazy. Joe had seen the group through so many awful times, the most recent of

155

which was Midnight's funeral three years before. It had been Joe who had come back from England and taken charge of the mess that everyone had been in. Joe made sure the funeral was arranged and got Rick through a lot of his misery, even talking Rick down from killing himself when he thought he'd never see Midnight again. Joe's own heart was shattered at having lost his best friend, and yet he'd been strong for everyone else. The idea that the pillar of strength they all counted on could crumble and possibly cease to exist was unfathomable.

The night Joe told Randy about the spot on his lungs, she called her brother, Donovan, to tell him. Donovan was just getting in when he received the call. He'd been out late on his case, and Randy had waited until she was sure Joe was asleep. To Donovan she fell apart, crying on the phone, telling him that she was terrified. Donovan finally drove over and talked to her late into the night, through to the next morning. Darrell was out of town, so they couldn't tell him. Randy would try to get ahold of him later the next day.

When Donovan finally dragged himself home, he was exhausted. He lay in his bed and found himself unable to sleep. Joe had always been this solid fortress of a man. When Randy started dating Joe, Donovan was a teenager. Joe had been larger than life to him. Donovan had honestly believed that Joe could do no wrong. Darrell had hated Joe at first, believing he had only been out for a piece of ass with Randy. Randy had only been twenty years old and very naive. She too had been bowled over by Joe, with his brooding light blue eyes, handsome grin, and English manners. There had been so much about Joe that was an enigma. He was handsome and confident, but by no means cocky. He was rich, unbelievably so, but he did a job that most people wouldn't do, risking his life daily.

Donovan had wanted to be a cop because Joe was a cop and he admired everything about the man. He couldn't believe that after everything Joe had been through and survived in his life, something so insidious as cancer could kill him. It was just not to be believed. But the facts were the facts. Joe had never managed to quit smoking, always taking the habit right back up during times of stress, which was pretty often in their business. There was a definite spot on one of his lungs, and he'd had a lingering cough for months. It had never gotten worse and become the pneumonia he was prone to, so Joe had figured it was just allergies or something.

What if it was cancer? What if they really lost Joe? Life wouldn't be the same—nothing would be the same.

Donovan's phone rang at 10:30 the next morning. He still hadn't managed to go to sleep.

"'Lo," he said tiredly.

"Donovan?" Erin said. He sounded so tired. "Did I wake you?"

"No, I'm awake. What's up?" Donovan was unaware that the entire department was alive with the rumors about Joe's illness.

"I just heard about Joe," Erin said. "Are you okay?"

Donovan was silent for a minute, debating—was he okay? No, he wasn't. Did he want to drag Erin down with him? No, he didn't. Did he need her? Yes, he did.

"Donovan?" Erin said, worried.

"I'm here. And no, I'm not okay," he said finally.

Erin bit her lip. She wanted to offer to go over to his house, but she didn't want to seem like she was grabbing any opportunity that came up. She just knew how much Joe meant to him; Jeanie had told her that Donovan practically worshiped Joe Sinclair.

"Erin?" Donovan said, because she'd been silent for so long.

"Yes?" she said, holding her breath.

"Can you come over?" he asked, sounding forlorn.

"I'll be there as fast as I can."

She was at his house a half hour later. He opened the door and she walked in. He looked tired, and he hadn't shaved or showered. Erin grimaced at how sad he looked.

"He'll be okay, Donovan," she said. "He has to be."

Donovan swallowed against the lump in his throat, nodding miserably.

"Come on." Erin took his hand and led him down the hall to his bedroom. She pushed him toward the bathroom, telling him to take a quick shower and that she'd make him something to eat. "Because I know you haven't eaten," she chided gently.

Donovan did as she told him, and was just shrugging into his bathrobe when she knocked on his bedroom door.

"You decent?" she asked from out in the hallway.

Donovan grinned. "Yeah."

She walked in, carrying a plate of scrambled eggs, toast, and Canadian bacon. She also had a glass of milk, knowing coffee would only keep him from sleeping.

Donovan made a face at the food. "I'm not really hungry, Erin…"

"You need to try to eat something. This is going to be a hard few days for you and your family. You need to keep your strength up."

Donovan took a deep breath, sighing deeply, then nodded and sat down on his bed to eat. When he'd had as much as he could handle, Erin took the plate and glass back to the kitchen. He was sitting staring off into space when she came back into the room.

Erin stood in front of him, looking down at him. "You okay?"

Donovan glanced up at her, his teal blue eyes caught by the light of the sun breaking through the clouds outside. Slowly he shook his head. Erin did the only thing she could think of, and that was to put her arms around him. He, in turn, did the same, wrapping his arms around her waist and resting his head against her mid-section. Erin stroked his hair.

"It'll be okay," she said, over and over again. When she felt his breathing start to even out, she gently pushed him back on the bed, picking his legs up and laying them out. She started to turn to go back into the kitchen and clean up, but his hand on her arm stopped her.

"Please don't go," he said softly.

"I'm not leaving, Donovan, I'm just—"

"Stay in here with me."

Erin nodded. "Okay. Whatever you want."

He took her wrist, pulling her down on the bed and moving over so she could lie down next to him. She rested with her back against the headboard. Donovan turned toward her, once again resting his head against her mid-section, one arm under the small of her back and the other wrapped around her waist. Erin stroked his hair soothingly until he fell asleep.

She sat there that morning thinking about how fragile life really was. Things that you counted on weren't always there forever. She was very glad she was getting the opportunity to be there for Donovan. She knew that it didn't mean anything; he needed someone and she was there—it was as simple as that. And she intended to be there for him as much as he'd let her be.

The phone rang an hour later. Donovan turned over sleepily and answered it.

"Curtis."

"Donny?" Randy said, sounding stressed, using the pet name she always had while they were growing up.

"Randy? What is it?" he asked, glancing at the clock as he sat up.

"He goes in for surgery at three o'clock today."

"I'll be there at two. Have you gotten ahold of Darrell yet?"

"No, I haven't. I can't get through."

"Okay, sis, don't worry about it. I'll get ahold of him."

"Thank you, Donny."

"Joe'll come through this—he's stronger than anyone I know."

"God, I hope so."

"I'll be there," Donovan repeated. They hung up a moment later.

Donovan turned to see that Erin was still sitting where she had been when he'd fallen asleep.

"Is everything okay?" she asked.

Donovan nodded. "Yeah. Joe's surgery is at three today."

"That's good—that's quick. The sooner you know what's happening, the better."

Donovan nodded again. "I'm going over there at two." He looked at her. "Will you come with me?"

"If you want me to, then yes, I will."

"Thanks," he said, smiling warmly.

Donovan spent the next hour trying to get ahold of his brother. He finally got through on Darrell's cell phone.

"Yeah?" Darrell answered, sounding irritated.

"Darrell, it's me," Donovan said, sitting with his back to the headboard. He was dressed now, in beige Dockers, a dark brown shirt, and his dark brown Doc Martens. Erin was sure he had no idea how handsome he looked, but she certainly noticed.

"What's up, Donovan? I'm on vacation, ya know."

"Look, Darrell, we need you back here as soon as possible."

"Why? What's going on now?" Darrell asked, assuming it was some new problem with the company.

"It's Joe. He's going in for surgery today at three."

"Surgery?" Darrell was starting to sound worried. "What the hell for?"

"They found a spot on one of his lungs," Donovan said, closing his eyes for a moment. It still felt like this whole thing was unreal.

"Fuck…" Darrell said, his usual eloquent self.

"Yeah…"

"He goes in at three?"

"Yeah."

"I won't make that." It was obvious from the tone of Darrell's voice that he was putting his mental schedule on overdrive. "But I'll be there tonight, Donovan, I promise. Tell Randy I'll be there."

"Thanks, man," Donovan said, happy that his usually recalcitrant brother knew when to be supportive.

Darrell had been stuck with the job of raising both Donovan and Randy when their parents left when Donovan was only nine. He hadn't always been the best at it, and there had been a number of things they'd all done without. Darrell hadn't always been the warmest man alive; working construction for years had hardened his body and in some cases his heart. When Joe had come into the picture, both Randy and Donovan had found themselves looking to Joe for the affection and warmth they'd missed from Darrell. Joe had become, in a way, a surrogate father to Donovan. There had been times when Darrell had resented the fact that Joe had come in and, in essence, taken over, but Joe had also given Darrell the opportunity to own his own business and be his own boss. For that Darrell had been grateful, and Joe and he had come to an understanding that Joe only wanted to love Randy, Donovan, and even Darrell with all he could give. They were now the family Joe had never really had, filling the void that had been left when Joe's parents had been killed.

"Is he going to make it?" Erin asked.

"Not for the surgery, but definitely tonight," Donovan said. He got off the bed, putting the phone back in its cradle. "Let's get going."

They drove over to the hospital and found the floor Joe was on. Donovan stopped at the nurses' station, asking what room he was in. The young nurse smiled warmly up at him before telling him. Outside the room, Donovan hesitated. He held back, trying to build up his confidence. Erin reached down and took his hand, looking up at him. He looked down at her, and he could see her faith in him. He gave her a small smile, squeezing her hand in a silent thank you. Still holding on, he walked to the door and took a deep breath.

"I'll be here when you come out," Erin said softly.

Donovan looked over at her and smiled. "Thanks."

Donovan walked into the room. Joe was sitting on the bed, looking edgy. Randy was standing next to him, her hand on his shoulder.

Joe looked up as the door opened, smiling when he saw Donovan, but it was apparent from the look in his eyes that he was nervous. It bothered Donovan to see Joe look nervous about anything, but he squashed the thought, knowing Joe needed support right now, not disillusioned hero worship.

"Hey, man," he said, walking over to his brother-in-law, his hand extended.

"Hey," Joe said, clasping Donovan's hand.

"Hey, sis," Donovan said, and leaned down to kiss Randy on the cheek. His other arm went around her waist to hug her. "So, what happens now?" he said, as if asking what the score was on the game.

"They're doing the biopsy," Randy said, her voice much stronger than it had been on the phone earlier that morning. "They took blood earlier to run some tests too."

"Yeah," Joe said, grinning. "I'm a bloody pin cushion."

"No, you're a guinea pig—deal with it," Randy said, smiling at him.

"Do I get lettuce if I'm good?"

"I'll give you something if you're good," Randy said, grinning mischievously.

Joe laughed, looking more relaxed again.

Donovan had to hand it to Randy—she was being outwardly very strong for Joe. It was exactly what his brother-in-law needed. Randy had grown up a lot in the years she'd been married to Joe. There had been a lot of really bad times, but they were far outweighed by the good.

"Darrell will be here tonight," he told them.

Randy nodded, looking relieved.

"Ah, babe…" Joe said, shaking his head. "You dragged Darrell back from his vacation?"

"He'd want to be here, Joe," Randy said.

"I didn't tell him to come," Donovan said. "He wanted to—Randy's right." He gave his brother-in-law a serious look. "You're our family, Joe, and you need us right now."

Joe nodded, understanding what Donovan was saying. He still felt sickened by the whole thing.

They spent the next hour trying to keep the conversation light, but there was no way to avoid the tension that was building. At 2:50 the nurse came in to start Joe's IV. Donovan and Randy stood back, and Joe kept his eyes on his wife's. He merely blinked when the nurse stuck the needle in his hand, his lips twitching when she couldn't find a suitable vein and had to move the needle around to get it in right. When the IV was in and taped into place in his hand, the nurse told him that he would be getting sleepy soon. She left the room.

"I'm gonna leave you two alone for a few," Donovan said. "I'll be here later when you wake up."

Joe nodded. "Thanks, man."

"You got it," Donovan said, grinning. He left.

Randy glanced at her husband, reaching down to brush his hair back off his forehead. "How are you doing?"

"I'm okay," he said, not really sounding like it.

"Getting sleepy yet?"

His eyes closed slowly, as if in answer to her question, but he opened them again. "I love you," he said softly.

"I love you too, Joseph Michael Sinclair," Randy said, with every ounce of conviction she had. "And you're going to be fine, okay?"

Joe nodded, his light blue eyes holding hers.

"Let go now, babe," Randy said quietly, seeing that he was fighting the medication that was trying to put him to sleep.

"Okay…" he breathed, closing his eyes.

Randy looked down at him with sudden tears in her eyes. She'd been so close to crying all morning, but had fought it down constantly. She had no idea what she'd do if they found cancer. If he actually ended up dying, she knew she couldn't take it. She'd always known that hers and Joe's was not the fiery romance like Rick and Midnight's, and she'd worried for a long time that Joe would miss that. But in the end, she'd realized that Joe needed her for what she wasn't, not what she was.

She wasn't a constant worry to him. Even though she'd fought to become a police officer, she'd figured out it wasn't really for her. And Joe had been relieved, because he had always been so afraid to lose her like he'd lost his parents, to violence. Things had become clear three years before when she'd almost been killed in a car accident. Her heart had actually stopped at one point in the hospital. Joe had told her he was sure he'd lost ten years on his life when she'd died, even for those few seconds.

They'd talked a lot after that, and she'd come to understand that he needed to know that the people he loved the most were safe. He couldn't control Midnight and her ways of doing things, and trying to would have changed Midnight into something she wasn't. Randy was what he wanted, what he'd always wanted and needed. They'd learned a lot of lessons over the years together, and the most important one was that they loved each other and needed each other for who they were. Their marriage was now at a place where they didn't have to talk to know what the other was thinking. They wanted the same things, they felt the same way about things, and when they didn't, they talked about it and came to a compromise. They didn't need the fights and arguments to know they were in love—they just knew they were.

Donovan stepped into the hallway. Erin was sitting just down the hall. He walked over to her and she stood up. Without a word, she reached up and hugged him. He smiled at the sweet gesture. When Randy came out a few minutes later, she walked down to where they stood.

"He okay?" Donovan asked. Randy nodded, looking drained. "Randy," Donovan said, gesturing to Erin. "This is Erin. She's a friend of mine."

"Nice to meet you," Randy said, smiling at the young woman and wondering remotely if Donovan was dating this girl now. Randy wasn't very happy with Jeanie for what she'd done. She knew that it had hit Donovan hard, but she had no idea how hard, because he'd hidden it from his sister.

"It's nice to meet you too," Erin said, smiling back at Randy. "I'm sorry about all you're going through right now. If I can help in any way, please let me know."

Randy nodded. "Thanks. I'm lucky, though—I have a pretty big extended family," she said, looking up at Donovan.

"Come on." Donovan put his arm around his sister. "I'm going to get you out of here for a little bit."

"Donny…" Randy said.

"Randy, you can't do anything right now but drive yourself crazy."

Randy nodded reluctantly. "Okay, but I can't guarantee that I'm good company."

"S'okay, sis, I'm used to that," Donovan said, grinning.

Randy elbowed him in the ribs. He laughed. Erin watched them. She'd never had siblings, so it was interesting to see how they related to each other.

Twenty minutes later they were at The Pit, a bar and grill owned by an ex-cop, Tom Ryan, the man responsible for Midnight's start in the department. As they sat down, Tom came over to the table, obviously in on one of his rare days there. He had since turned the business over to his nephew, but still came in every so often to "keep his hand in matters."

Tom greeted Randy warmly. "How's Joe?" he asked, having heard about the whole thing from some of the Gang as well as from Midnight.

"He's in surgery right now," Randy said soberly.

"And you look like you need a good meal," Tom said with a critical, fatherly eye. He looked at Donovan. "And you, young man, you look like hell. When's the last time you had a decent meal? You look like you've lost about twenty pounds!" He reached over and hugged Donovan, whose grimace was lost against the older man's shoulder.

To Donovan's dismay, Randy was giving him an appraising look when he glanced over at her. *Oh crap,* Donovan thought.

"Tom, this is Erin Shandley," Donovan said. "Erin, this is Tom Ryan."

"Nice to meet you," Erin said, noticing that the older man was appraising her too.

"You need to eat too," Ryan said, giving her a jokingly stern look. "What is wrong with you people?" He went back to his kitchen then.

They sat down at the table, and Donovan noticed, much to his dismay, that Randy was still eyeing him.

"Tom's right, Donny. You have lost weight," she said.

"Sis, please?"

"This stuff with Jeanie was worse on you than you told me, wasn't it?" Randy had a mother's intuition where Donovan was concerned.

Donovan didn't say anything for a few moments, then sighed, leaning back in the booth and putting his arm up on the back of the seat behind Erin. "Yeah, okay, it sucks."

"She's not worth it," Randy said, narrowing her eyes.

"Doesn't seem to matter."

"Donny... please just tell me that you're taking care of yourself now."

"I am," he answered too quickly.

"Bullshit."

"I will, okay?" he said, trying to end the conversation.

Randy gave him a long, measured look, then nodded. She turned to Erin. "So, do you work at the department?"

"Yes," Erin said, having to keep herself from calling Randy "ma'am," sure the other woman wouldn't like it. "I work in the secretarial pool."

"Don't say that like it's a bad thing," Randy said, grinning.

"Randy started out at the department as Joe's secretary," Donovan said.

"Oh my God, really?" Erin said, her blue eyes shining.

Randy laughed softly. "Oh yes."

"Is that how you two got together?" Erin asked, looking excited.

"Well, it's how we met." Randy glanced at Donovan, who had begun shaking his head. "What?"

"Oh, it's Erin," Donovan said. "She loves a good love story."

"Can I help it?" Erin said, giving him an exasperated look. "I was deprived of romance novels as a child!"

"Well, Randy and Joe are a classic romance story," Donovan said, smiling over at his sister. "Tell her, Randy."

"She doesn't want to hear that story," Randy said, shaking her head.

"Yes, I do—please?" Erin said, her bright eyes shining, like a kid at Christmas.

"Well…" Randy said. "Okay. I met Joe the very first day I started at the department. I was hired to be the secretary for FORS. Midnight had already impressed me with her easygoing way of doing things. But when I saw Joe the first time, I was speechless. He was so handsome, and such an obvious bad boy."

"And Joe looks exactly like he did then today," Donovan put in.

"Yes, he does," Randy said, smiling fondly. "The handsome devil. Anyway, there were a lot of things going on then, but Joe was always very sweet to me. It went against everything he seemed to be on the outside. He looked like a rough, tough street cop, but I discovered that he really had a heart of gold…" Randy went on to tell Erin the whole story about how she and Joe had gotten together, with Joe being shot and almost killed, and Randy having been the one to take care of him once he'd gotten out of the hospital.

Erin listened avidly, barely touching her lunch when it came. Donovan watched his sister's face light up as she retold how she and Joe met and the day they were married. He knew this was helping Randy forget, just for the moment at least, about worrying about Joe. He was very grateful to Erin for doing this for his sister, even if she didn't realize what she was doing.

When they were done with lunch, Donovan excused himself to go to the restroom. Randy grabbed the opportunity to reach across the table and take Erin's hand.

"Now, tell me the truth—how is he really handling this stuff with Jeanie?"

Erin hesitated, not wanting to rat Donovan out but knowing that his sister was concerned for his well-being. "He's okay now, I think," she said carefully.

"But he wasn't before, right?"

"No," Erin said, shaking her head. "But he's a lot better now, Randy, really."

Randy tilted her head to the side. "I think you might have something to do with that."

Erin's eyes widened, then she shook her head. "No, ma'am, I don't think so."

"Erin, don't call me ma'am. I'm only thirty-three," Randy said, grinning, then gave the young girl another appraising look. "Yeah, I think you're helping him more than even you realize."

"Randy, you don't understand—Jeanie was my friend."

"Was?" Randy asked, picking up on the subtle difference.

Erin grimaced. "Yes. I don't like what she did to Donovan either. She had everything and she gave it up."

Randy smiled fondly. "You're in love with him, aren't you?"

Erin's eyes widened to saucers. She looked like a scared doe caught in the headlights, but she shook her head again. "No... I'm just, I like him, he's a very sweet guy, and—"

"And you're in love with him, Erin."

"Why do you think that?" Erin asked, looking around like she was guilty of something and praying she wouldn't get caught.

"Because you said Jeanie had 'everything' and gave it up. You think of my brother as everything."

Erin bit her lip, not realizing that she'd said it that way. God, what if she was in love with Donovan? Was she crazy? Donovan was in love with Jeanie—everyone knew that. She paled at the thought

171

that Randy was right.

"Are you okay?" Donovan asked as he walked up to the table. He touched her arm and Erin jumped. "Jesus, Erin," he said, sounding alarmed. "Are you okay?"

Erin glanced over at Randy and saw that the other woman was smiling happily. She nodded. "Yes, I'm okay. I was just thinking about something. I'm okay."

"Okay…" Donovan said, looking from Erin to his sister and thinking that he was missing something.

"Come on," Randy said, standing up. "I want to get back to the hospital. I want to make sure I'm there when Joe wakes up."

They thanked Tom, who, as usual, refused to let them pay, and left The Pit.

The next hour passed slowly. Randy paced; Donovan and Erin sat and waited. Sometimes Donovan would get up and pace with his sister. At five o'clock the Gang started to arrive. Erin watched as people walked up; she knew all about the Gang too.

They were the department celebrities. Dave Dibbins arrived first, with a very beautiful blond woman. Donovan told her that she was Susan Endicott, Rick Debenshire's niece. Dave walked over to Randy, taking her in his arms and hugging her, whispering something to her that made her nod. Susan hugged Randy too. Dave came over to Donovan, extending his hand to the younger man. Donovan shook it and introduced Erin. Dave smiled at the young woman and warmly said, "Good to meet you." He went to sit down in one of the chairs in the waiting room, moving gingerly. Susan sat with him, whispering something to him, to which he shook his head.

The next to arrive were Midnight and Kyle Masterson. Midnight hugged Randy, then Kyle did too. Midnight walked over to Donovan, who stood to hug her. Kyle and Donovan shook hands. Midnight looked at Erin, smiling, then glanced at Donovan.

"Oh, sorry, Chief, this is Erin Shandley. Erin, this is Midnight."

Erin had stood when Midnight came over, knowing exactly who she was. She tried her best not to be bowled over by the fact that Donovan was on a first-name basis with the Chief of Police.

"Erin?" Midnight repeated. "You're going to be on our inventory team, aren't you?" She looked at Kyle, who nodded in confirmation. "Nice to meet you," Midnight said then, smiling.

"You too, ma'am," Erin said, her voice a little choked. Midnight Chevalier knew who she was?

"Call me Midnight. If you're here, you're part of the family now."

"Ma'am?" Erin queried, her voice cracking slightly.

Midnight nodded to Donovan. "If Pony brought you with him at a time like this, you're important to him—that makes you family."

Erin was stunned, not having realized that Donovan bringing her with him was that big of a deal. She looked at him, and he nodded. Erin couldn't even formulate a response to that; she only nodded numbly. Midnight went over to talk to Dave and took a seat. Kyle followed.

Christian, Stevie, and Rhiannon were next. Rhiannon headed over to talk to Kyle, and Stevie went with her after having a couple of words with Randy. Christian gave Randy a hug, talking to her for a long few minutes. Randy nodded a few times, and it was obvious she was crying a bit, but she smiled then, even laughing a little as she

173

reached up and hugged Christian. Erin looked at Donovan and saw that he was smiling and nodding, obviously pleased with the other man for having made his sister laugh. Christian came over, clasping Donovan's hand.

"Hey, man, how you holding up?" Christian asked, aware of Jeanie's desertion of Donovan too.

"I'm alright, Blue, thanks."

The Englishman's light blue eyes turned on Erin then. She stared up at him, dumbfounded for a moment. He was too handsome to be believed.

"Oh, damn," Donovan said. "Sorry. This is Erin—Erin, this is Blue. If you're on the inventory team, you'll be working with him."

Erin nodded, smiling slightly up at the Englishman, not sure what to say.

Christian motioned to one of the women he'd come with, and she walked over.

"This is Stevie O'Neil," Christian said, gesturing to the woman with rich auburn hair and beautiful green eyes. "Stevie, this is Donovan Curtis, Joe's brother-in-law, and this is Erin. Apparently Erin will be working on the inventory with us."

Stevie extended her hand to Donovan, nodding respectfully to him. "I hear you're a pretty good narc," she said, grinning.

Donovan looked surprised. He knew this was the Stevie O'Neil that had just been brought back from helping to take down Marco Tiempo. "I hear you're pretty good at UC too."

Stevie laughed lightly, shrugging. Then she turned to Erin; the young girl looked absolutely overwhelmed. Stevie was too, but she hid it a lot better.

"Hi," Stevie said, extending her hand.

"Hi," Erin replied, smiling at Stevie's simple greeting.

Rick Debenshire walked up then, going to Randy and hugging her. Then he went to his wife, nodding to Donovan as he walked by. He knelt down in front of Midnight, talking to her for a few minutes. Erin found she couldn't take her eyes off them. It was like seeing legends in person. She'd heard all the stories about Midnight and Rick Debenshire. Their fiery fights in the office, their just-as-fiery love for each other. She too had heard about the funeral for Midnight three years before. Every woman in the secretarial pool was in love with the Debenshire romance.

As she watched, Rick stood up and walked over to Randy. To her utter dismay, Rick Debenshire's eyes fell on her even as she continued to watch him. Worse still, he turned and came over to where she sat with Donovan; she vaguely heard Midnight say, "Richard!" But Rick's deep blue eyes were staring down at her. If she'd known him better, she'd have known the glint in them was humor, but she was terrified.

"Hey, Rick," Donovan said easily.

"Hey, Pony," Rick said smoothly, his eyes shifting to Donovan while they shook hands. He turned back to Erin.

"Rick, this is Erin. Erin, this is Rick Debenshire," Donovan said, then with a sly grin added, "Midnight's husband."

Rick gave Donovan a narrow look. "Watch it, Pony, or you'll be back on patrol before the end of the day."

Donovan laughed at the threat. "Sir, yes, sir."

175

Rick canted his head to the side to look at Erin. "Nice to meet you."

Erin's eyes were wide; she didn't know what was going on, but she felt like a really big dork at that point.

"Richard Debenshire, stop hassling that kid," Midnight said, coming over to stand beside her husband.

Rick glanced at his wife with feigned innocence, then looked back at Erin. "Am I hassling you?" he asked, the beginnings of a grin on his lips.

"Um, no, sir," Erin said. She saw Donovan giving Rick a dirty look before turning back to her, shaking his head.

"See?" Rick said.

"I'm sorry, Erin," Midnight said, giving her husband a vile look. "Sometimes they're like big kids—you can't tell them *anything* without causing a stir." She swatted Rick on the arm, and he laughed.

Erin wasn't sure what Midnight had told Rick that would cause him to come over and talk to her, but she wasn't sure she wanted to know either. She had no idea that Rick found it quite adorable that she had this wide-eyed awed look on her face. She also had no idea that Midnight had told him that she thought Donovan had moved on and that Erin was his new lady. Rick had a soft spot in his heart for Donovan, considering Donovan had almost been killed trying to rescue Midnight when her car had blown up three years before. He'd come to think of Donovan as the little brother he had never had. For that reason, he liked to give the younger man a hard time about the ladies he dated. Like the others, Rick wasn't pleased with the way things had turned out with Jeanie. It didn't occur to Erin that Randy had just told Rick she was sure Erin was in love with Donovan.

Rick knelt down in front of her, smiling warmly. He took her hand in his with deliberate gentleness. "Don't worry, most of us don't bite," he said, grinning.

"Or they've had their rabies shots, if they do," Donovan put in. Rick laughed.

"It's nice to meet you, sir," Erin said, biting her lower lip.

"It's Rick, not sir," Rick said, smiling now. "And loosen up, Erin—it could be a long night."

Erin nodded, still not sure what had caused this kind of attention from a man like Rick Debenshire. Midnight dragged him back over to where they'd been sitting. Erin watched as she sat back down in the chair and Rick moved to sit on the floor in front of her. Midnight's hand reached down to touch his shoulder, and his hand automatically came up to hold hers.

A little while later, Tiny Ako, his wife, Jessica, Spider Nguyen, and his wife, Tammy, arrived. Introductions were made all around. Kana arrived last, explaining she'd been in the middle of an investigation when she'd gotten the page.

It was two more hours before the doctor came out to talk to Randy. Midnight, Rick, Dave, Spider, Tiny, and Kana all went over to stand behind her. The doctor explained that Joe was resting, that the surgery had gone fine. He also explained that it hadn't really taken that long, that he'd been bumped by an emergency.

"When can I see him?" Randy asked.

"In another couple of hours," the doctor said. "He's just coming out of the anesthetic now."

Randy nodded. "And how long will it take to get the results?" she asked, her voice trembling. Rick reached forward, clasping her shoulder. Midnight reached out to take Randy's hand.

"It'll be at least three days, possibly four. I'm asking the lab to rush things," the doctor said, feeling a bit intimidated by the people standing around him. He knew these people—they'd been here a number of times before—but they never ceased to make him feel uneasy, especially if he didn't have good news for them.

Randy nodded, closing her eyes. Four more days of this?

"Four days?" Rick said, sounding disgusted. "They have to wait four days? You got to be kidding me."

"I'm sorry, sir."

"The hell you are—it's not you doing the waiting," Spider muttered.

"Yeah, easy for you to say," Tiny put in.

"Four days and that's a rush?" Dave mused.

"Okay, okay," Midnight said, taking charge as the doctor started to pale at the onslaught. "Tone it down, people. The doctor said he's rushing it—that's the best we can do." She squeezed Randy's hand. "We'll be with you the whole time, Randy. Don't worry."

Randy nodded. "Thanks, guys," she said, tears in her eyes.

Darrell showed up just then, calling his sister's name. Randy turned and was caught up in a bear hug. Darrell nodded to the Gang as he embraced his sister. Donovan came to join them, shaking Darrell's hand.

Erin watched all of it, amazed that people from such different backgrounds and lifestyles could bond the way these people had. She gained a new respect for the Gang that night, as did Stevie O'Neil. It was one thing to hear about a group like this over the years, quite another to witness the way they backed each other up.

As it turned out, they all stayed until Joe was awake and back in his room. Then they went in pairs to see him. Joe was in good spirits, but it was obvious he was tired, so everyone kept the visits short.

Erin went home thinking about everything she'd seen, and feeling more determined than ever to help Donovan in any way she could. She lay in the dark, after putting her son to bed, thinking about what Randy had said. Was she really in love with Donovan? How was that possible? Deep in her heart, though, she knew Randy was right. Donovan was impossible to resist, and having him actually need her had cemented it for her. She knew that he didn't love her, but she realized too that he didn't have to. She could be there for him right now, and if they remained friends, that was okay. As it was, she felt like a horrible person for falling in love with her friend's man. Because no matter what Jeanie had done to Donovan, he was still Jeanie's man. He loved her.

The following morning, Saturday, Erin's roommate was taking Bobby to the zoo so Erin could have a day off to herself. Erin got dressed in shorts, a T-shirt, and tennis shoes, pulling her hair up in a ponytail. She planned to do some shopping; Bobby needed some new summer clothes and some more activity books to practice with. She decided she'd stop by Donovan's to make sure he was okay, telling herself that if she called him he could lie about how he was doing. The truth was, she wanted to see him again.

She buzzed the intercom at his front door. He answered after a few long moments and buzzed her in.

"Donovan?" she said, standing at the end of the hallway.

"Down here," he called.

She walked down the hall into his bedroom. He was still lying in bed, on his stomach, his arms clutched around the pillow under his head. She noted he wasn't wearing a shirt, and found it necessary to look elsewhere; otherwise she knew she'd stare.

"You okay?" she asked, noting it was noon.

"Uh-huh," he said, his voice muffled by the pillow.

"You sure?" She went over to the bed, looking down at the side of his face.

He opened one eye, looking up at her. "No."

Erin sat down on the bed, concerned. Donovan turned over on his back, looking at her. Her eyes were drawn to his chest. *Oh my God*, was all she could think. He was so handsome, and seeing him the way he was right then, his hair tousled from sleep, his teal blue eyes shining up at her, his bare chest...

Donovan caught the look on Erin's face. He was almost sure he saw desire in her eyes, but she looked away too quickly for him to be totally sure. Randy had told him the night before that she thought Erin was really sweet. He'd told her that Erin was just a friend. Randy's reply had been, "Well, maybe you should look at changing that."

She had refused to elaborate, but the comment had Donovan wondering now.

He sat up, bringing him closer to her.

"So what brings you here?" he asked warmly.

"I just wanted to make sure you were okay," Erin said, far too quickly, her eyes still averted, her head actually turned to the side.

Donovan narrowed his eyes. "Why won't you look at me?"

She turned her head and looked him in the eyes, surprised that he'd said anything. "I—" she began, stopping herself because she couldn't think of anything to say.

"You what, Erin?" he asked, his teal eyes looking down into hers.

"Nothing, Donovan," she said, turning her head away again. "I just stopped by to make sure you were okay."

She moved to stand up. His hand stopped her. She turned her head to look at him, just as he tugged her back on the bed. Before she knew what was happening, his lips were on hers. Her body lit up instantly, but her mind reeled at the thought that she was being kissed by her friend's man. *This is not right!* her mind screamed at her. To her amazement, she found herself pushing him away. "Donovan, this isn't right. We can't."

"Why?" Donovan asked, his lips still far too close, his eyes searching hers.

Erin turned her head away. "Because you're in love with Jeanie—we both know that, and she's my friend, and I just... I don't think it's a good idea."

Donovan moved away, and she looked up to catch the closed look on his face.

"Donovan?" she said, worried that he had closed up so quickly.

"It's okay," he said, sounding like it was far from okay. "I understand."

"We're friends, Donovan. I just think we need to stay that way," she said, trying to make sure he did understand, but he was nodding, his eyes pointedly averted from hers. "Donovan…" she said beseechingly, but he wouldn't look at her again.

"It's cool, Erin, okay?" he said, sounding irritated now.

"No, it's not okay. What is it?"

"Look," he said, moving to sit up straighter, pulling his knees up to his chest, draping his arms over them. "You don't want me, that's fine—it's cool. I'm sorry I kissed you."

"Oh my God, Donovan. You don't seriously think that, do you?" Donovan looked back at her, and it was obvious that he did. "You are so wrong," she said, shaking her head. Donovan's expression didn't change. "I have lain awake nights thinking about you. Jesus, my body is still screaming bloody murder at me for stopping. Okay?"

He just stared back at her for a long moment, assessing this time, and then a slow grin started on his lips. He reached out and touched her cheek, sliding his hand down to her neck, caressing her. Her eyes closed as a thrill ran through her. When she opened them again, she saw that his expression had changed.

"Donovan, no," she managed to say, right before he pulled her toward him again, his lips taking possession of hers. His kiss was stronger this time, much less tentative, and her mind ceased working for a moment. Her body took over in that time, her arms going around his neck as he pulled her across his lap, his lips still on hers. He kissed her, making her feel like her lips were on fire, along with the rest of her body. She wanted to protest when he pulled her shirt out of her shorts and over her head, but she could only groan as his thumbs brushed over her breasts through her satin bra. Her body refused to allow her to move away from him this time.

Donovan sensed her surrender, and kissed her harder, wanting to take what she would give. He knew he was pushing her, but he wanted to feel someone wanting him again—he needed it. Every moan, sigh, and gasp restored his soul a little more. When his body slid into hers, she cried out his name, grasping his shoulders. He knew what he was doing, he knew he was taking shelter in the warmth of her embrace. He refused to allow himself to think farther than that. He cared about her, he did—he didn't love her, but she knew that. But he wanted her, and she wanted him, and that was enough right now.

CHAPTER 6

The morning after Joe's surgery, Susan got the children off to school then went by Dave's house to check on him. She knew he had overdone it the night before at the hospital, sitting in that chair all that time. She wanted to make sure he wasn't in dire shape again. She rang the bell, and as usual he buzzed her in. Walking down the hall, she heard the water running in his bathroom. When she went into his room she saw that his bathroom door was open, so she assumed it was safe to approach. *Safe is such a broad term,* she thought as she caught a glimpse of Dave standing at the bathroom sink, shaving. He wore a pair of faded jeans and nothing else. His gold cross hung around his neck, shining in the bathroom light. He looked tanned, strong, and healthy. His blue eyes caught hers in the reflection.

"Good morning," he said warmly.

"Well," Susan said, smiling at him, "I guess you don't need me anymore."

Dave grinned. "Now why do you say that?"

"You're standing perfectly upright, Mr. Dibbins," she said, gesturing to his back.

"Well, that's true," he said, continuing to shave. "But that doesn't mean I couldn't relapse suddenly." The twinkle in his eyes was mischievous.

"Oh, I see…" Susan said, leaning against the doorjamb and

crossing her arms in front of her chest. "You're saying you might fake a relapse?"

Dave laughed. "I might."

"And what would the purpose in that be?" Susan asked, sounding very English.

Dave's eyes looked straight into hers through the reflection in the mirror, his face serious. "To keep you near me."

Susan said nothing for a long moment, her breath catching in her throat. As she searched for something to say, Dave reached for a towel, wiping his face. He turned to her, leaning his hip against the sink, watching her eyes, but he said nothing, just waited for her to respond.

"I don't think a relapse will be necessary for that, David," Susan said finally, her voice soft.

Dave grinned. "Good, I hate lying around for long periods of time."

Susan bit her lip, not knowing what to say or how to act right then. Dave stood and gestured for her to precede him out of the bathroom. She turned and walked into his room. She sat down on the bed, watched as he pulled on a beige T-shirt and sat down on the chair next to his dresser to put on his shoes and socks. His sandy-brown hair fell across his forehead as he leaned down, so when he looked up at her it was through a veil of hair. His blue eyes seemed to shine.

"So what are you up to today? Besides checking on the invalid," he said, gesturing to himself.

"Well, the children are in school until three, so I was planning to go over and see Joe."

"Then we can go together," he said, standing up. "If that's okay?"

"Of course," Susan said, smiling.

She watched in fascination as he shrugged into his shoulder holster, making adjustments to the leather to make it comfortable. Then he loaded his ammunition clip and slid it into the gun he carried, pulling back the slide to chamber a round. He put two more clips into the other side of the holster and then picked up his badge, clipping it to his belt. He walked over to his closet and pulled out a black shirt with a beige-and-burgundy Hawaiian pattern at the bottom. Dave embodied the term casual cool. There was nothing about him to suggest he was a police officer except the gun and the badge, which were nicely hidden under the shirt. Susan realized she was one of probably millions of women who found men with guns very sexy. She hadn't really realized she felt that way until just then, watching Dave handle the weapon so expertly and with such ease. With Dave's easygoing, gentle ways and kind demeanor, she could so easily forget he was really an undercover narcotics officer.

"You ready?" he asked.

"Yes," she said, and at his gesture, went out of the room ahead of him.

She was wearing cream linen slacks, a light green short-sleeved sweater, and brown suede deck shoes. She was the picture of casual elegance, and as Dave followed her down the hall, he wondered what had possessed him to make a pass at her. He certainly found her attractive. There was no denying that Susan Endicott was lovely, with her luxurious blond hair, her smooth skin, her sapphire blue eyes, and a nicely shaped body that could keep a man up nights. But she was also about sixteen years younger than him. And as they'd discussed, Susan wasn't the kind of woman one had a casual affair with. Besides the fact that she was the niece of Rick Debenshire, who would more than likely put him in the ground for even thinking about her, Susan Endicott was on such a different level than he was.

Susan was from a good family with money. Dave hadn't even seen his parents since he'd busted them for having a meth lab in their trailer six years ago. He came from what would be considered the dregs of society. Susan had been educated in the best schools in England; Dave had been lucky to finish high school before going on to be a drug-dealing gang leader. She was a proper English nanny; he was an undercover narc in the seedy world of drugs, guns, and money. They were about as opposite as two people could get.

But her sweet, gentle personality had captured his attention. He'd never believed that he'd be interested in a woman like her, but he was—he definitely was. He knew, too, that he was daring some serious fire from the Debenshire household. Dave remembered well what had happened to Christian Collins when Rick found out about his dalliance with Susan. Collins had taken a fairly nasty right cross that had bruised for a week. And Midnight had been there to pull Rick off. Dave wasn't altogether sure she wouldn't help Rick beat the shit out of him if he trifled with Susan. He knew that Midnight liked him, on a professional and friendship level, but it was an altogether different story when her sweet young niece was involved. Midnight could be just as protective as any mother bear when it came to her relatives. God knew Rick was going to kill him.

All of this went through Dave's mind as he followed Susan out to his car. He opened the passenger door for her, smiling at her as she glanced up at him. The drive to the hospital was quick, so they didn't really talk much. The radio played in the car. He did ask her what she usually listened to; she shrugged, saying that she pretty much listened to everything.

"My uncle and Joe listen to rock, Christian listens to alternative music and some rock, and my aunt listens to top-40 music, so I end up hearing a lot of different things and liking some of everything."

"Go ahead and put on whatever you want then," he said, gesturing to his radio.

Susan found a top-40 station and left it there.

The Backstreet Boys came on with "More Than That." Dave found it pretty ironic, considering the direction of his thoughts and Susan's current situation. He wondered if she was really listening to the words. She was. The lyrics talked about how he could be better for her than her current love was. It was an interesting thought.

As the song ended, they reached the hospital. Dave parked and got out, coming around to open Susan's door for her. She was still surprised when he did that. It was old-fashioned, but quite endearing. The words to the song had indeed stuck in her head. She thought about them as they walked into the hospital. She did know that she was probably wasting her time waiting for Christian, and had begun to realize that even though she loved him, that didn't necessarily mean forever for them. It was difficult to forget the dream she'd had of marrying Christian someday, but she also found herself thinking about Dave a lot these days.

She didn't think it was love or anything, but she knew she wanted to spend more time with him to get more insight into him. Every minute she was with him, she found out something new, about him and the people that had been her "family" for years. It was very exciting in many ways. She actually felt included in their world now. She equated it to finally being able to sit at the table with the adults and talk to them on their level, and hear the stories they'd always thought her too young or innocent for.

And then there was that undeniable physical attraction she had to Dave. That in and of itself was something she felt a definite need to explore. Christian had taught her about desire and taking what you wanted when it came to sex. It wasn't always as easy as that, certainly not as easy for her as it was for Christian, but it gave her enough understanding to know that she was sexually attracted to Dave Dibbins. It also gave her the courage to pursue that attraction to its end—just not necessarily the courage to make the first move. She'd been happily surprised by his admission of wanting to spend time with her that morning. It had made her feel like she wasn't crazy or alone in this attraction she felt for him.

When they got upstairs to Joe's room, Dave knocked lightly. It was Randy's voice that called for them to come in. Joe was sitting up in the bed, wearing his jeans and no shirt; there was a small bandage on his upper torso. That was the only evidence that he'd had surgery. He did look tired, Susan noted, but she imagined that the very stress of what was happening would cause that.

Dave walked over and the two men shook hands. "Good to see you back to generally normal," Dave said, his tone friendly, a mischievous glint in his eyes.

"Has he ever been normal?" Randy said, picking up on the joke easily enough.

Dave looked thoughtful for a moment, then shook his head. "Not to my knowledge."

"Yeah, fuck you," Joe said, grinning.

Dave laughed, as did Randy and Susan.

"How are you feeling, Dave?" Randy asked, knowing that he'd been hurt.

"I'm okay. Susan's been helping a lot, making sure I don't make human-pretzel status."

"He gives you too hard a time, Susan, just hide his surf board," Joe said.

"Hey, that's low," Dave said, scowling at Joe.

"That or the keys to the Charger," Randy added.

"I'm leaving," Dave said, his face serious. He laughed a moment later, ruining the effect.

"Actually, he's a pretty good patient," Susan said. "Almost better than the children."

Dave looked over at her. "Am I being compared to children now?"

"If the shoe fits…" Joe muttered.

"Don't make me shoot you, Sinclair," Dave growled, grinning all the while.

"Seriously, man," Joe said. "How's the back?"

"It's good, Joe, no worries. I'm in good hands," Dave said, gesturing to Susan.

Joe nodded, his eyes showing nothing of what he was thinking. He'd noted that Susan was with Dave the night before, and now today she was with him again. Something was going on there; he could feel it. He brought it up with Midnight later that morning when she came to see him.

"You think what?" Midnight asked, looking at him like he was nuts.

"I'm tellin' you, Night, there's something goin' on there."

"Joe," Midnight said, shaking her head at him, "I asked Susan to keep an eye on Dave after he rolled that car. You know he lives alone, and I know he'd just self-medicate if someone wasn't there to keep an eye on him. There's nothing going on." She rolled her eyes. "Jesus, you're turning into a suspicious old lady!"

Joe just shook his head. "I'm tellin' ya—but don't believe me, you'll see for yourself."

"You know what kind of woman Dave dates—Susan's not even close to being his type. She is so much younger than him, practically a kid!"

Joe glowered at her. "Randy's a lot younger than me, Night. And Susan's not a kid anymore."

Midnight's expression changed then; she realized she'd always seen Susan as the little girl she'd been years before, not the woman she was now. Was it possible? Joe's instincts were usually right on. Jesus... Dave and Susan? No way! Dave usually went for the type of woman that wouldn't cling; Susan was about as clingy as they got. She was a good girl, not Dave's type at all... Good lord, Rick would have a fit!

"Look, Joe," Midnight said, giving him a serious look. "Don't bring this up with Rick, please, okay? I don't want him killing my best narc over your suspicions."

Joe laughed. She was right; Rick would probably come unglued, considering how he'd reacted to Christian and Susan. If Susan was seeing Dave, she'd just stepped up in players. Dave was a master at it—everyone knew that, including Rick.

"Promise me, Sinclair. I'm serious," Midnight said.

"I promise, I promise," Joe said, holding up his right hand. "But Rick's pretty intuitive, so you better keep Susan away from him, and Dibbs for that matter."

Midnight nodded, blowing her breath out. "I know, I know."

Unaware they were being discussed, Dave and Susan were driving toward the beach. Dave had asked if she minded a trip to the ocean, saying that he was starting to have withdrawals. She had laughed and said it sounded good.

Out of habit, Dave drove to his favorite place, a little-used area of Imperial Beach where the rocks ran right up to the apartments. He'd been going to the spot since he was a kid. He didn't know how many times he'd hitchhiked or ridden his bike there to sit and watch the waves come in, but when he was even the slightest bit troubled, that was where he went.

He parked the car, getting out and opening the door for Susan. She looked around. She had a feeling this was something special to him. It was certainly what one would consider a "date" spot. As they walked across the road, he took her hand. Susan felt a thrill go through her at the physical contact. He walked over to an area where the fence was down, helping her step over it, then proceeded to help her up onto the tall rocks nearby. It reminded her of the area in La Jolla Christian had taken her to. This wasn't as high up, but it was still very nice.

"I used to come here a lot as a kid," Dave explained as he pulled her up the last rock.

"Really?"

"Yeah, I lived about two miles from here," he said, looking a little chagrined.

"You did?" she asked, surprised.

"Yeah." He gazed out over the ocean, his eyes lit by the reflection.

"Will you show me?"

Dave looked down at her. "I…" he started, then shook his head. "I don't think so."

"Why?" she asked, surprised by his refusal.

Again he glanced at her, then looked back out over the ocean and shrugged. "Susan, where I grew up… it's not really anything to be proud of."

Susan's expression told him she was trying to understand, but didn't.

"I grew up in a trailer park. In a dump, basically," he said, feeling defensive all of a sudden.

"David, it doesn't matter where you grew up," she said softly.

"No?" he said, sounding cynical for the first time since she'd gotten to know him.

"No," she said, her conviction obvious. "You are who you are now, not where you grew up. You had no control over that."

Dave saw her sincerity in her eyes. He pursed his lips, considering the idea of showing her the rat hole he'd grown up in. Finally he nodded. "Okay, if you think you want to see it, I'll show you."

"I do want to see," she said, reaching out to touch his arm. "But I want you to tell me about this place first."

He looked down at her for a long moment, not used to anyone wanting to know about him in depth. Then he pointed to the pier in the distance. "I used to hang out there," he said. "But there was an old guy that fished there that hassled me all the time, so I wandered out to these rocks and started coming here when I wanted to be alone and just think."

Susan nodded, waiting for him to continue.

"So whenever things got too hot at home, I'd jump on my bike and come here. It was a good long ride, which usually got rid of most of my anger, and then I'd just sit here and watch the waves come in for the night. It always calmed me down."

"What would happen at home to make it 'hot'?"

Dave shrugged. "Well, pretty much anything. My dad was a total loser, never kept a job for long, just long enough to make the rent or go on unemployment. So whenever he'd lose a job, my mother would start in on him about what a loser he was. Then she'd start in on me about not becoming a loser like my dad, all that shit…" His voice trailed off as he looked out over the ocean again, remembering those days. He'd wanted to scream at his mother so many times, but he'd left instead.

"My lord, she said all that to you?" Susan looked shocked.

"Oh, she said a lot worse, trust me."

"Like what?"

Dave grimaced. "A lot of things a young lady from a good family shouldn't hear."

"David..."

"Susan, trust me. It was things you would never have heard in your household," he said, his eyes roving over the waves again.

Susan touched his cheek. "Tell me, please," she said softly when he looked down at her.

"She'd tell me things like how I needed to keep my, ah, well, my... manhood in my pants... stuff like that," he said, looking genuinely embarrassed.

Susan nodded, understanding his chagrin, but assuring him that it wasn't that shocking.

Dave sat on the rock, pulling her down with him. "See that?" he said, pointing to a spot in the water that was smooth compared to the rest of the ocean.

Susan turned in the direction he was pointing, causing her to move almost in front of him. "Yes."

"That's a rip tide, and..." He looked down the beach, nodding and pointing at a red truck driving slowly along the sand. "That's the lifeguard putting out warnings."

"What does a rip tide do?" Susan asked.

"Well, it's an alternate current to the normal push and pull of the ocean. It can pull you under and hold you down until you die."

"Good lord," Susan said, looking worried. "And you surf in these?"

Dave grinned. "Well, they're usually lower to the bottom of the ocean, and I'm usually on the surface on my board, so it's not really an issue."

"Oh," she said, looking relieved.

A breeze blew up then, gusting her hair, which was loose except for a braid that pulled the front of it off her face. Susan shivered. Even though it was late spring, it was still chilly out at the shore.

"Cold?" Dave asked.

"A little."

"We could go back to the car," he said, starting to stand.

"No," Susan said quickly. "I'm okay, David, really."

Dave looked doubtful for a moment, then nodded.

"Tell me more about this place," she said.

Dave grinned. He'd never actually brought anyone out here; this was all new to him. He leaned far over, looking down the side of the rock. "Yep, it's still here," he said.

"What is?" Susan asked, leaning over to try and see what he was looking at. His hands caught her around the waist, because he was worried she'd lean too far. Susan looked at him for a long moment; he only smiled, setting her back a bit on the rock. He jumped down, then held out his hand. She took it, and he helped her hop down from the rock, then grabbed her waist to lower her to the ground.

He pointed to a place on the rock where there was writing: "IB Bad Boy."

"Your gang?" she asked.

"No, me. I was that long before I was the leader of the Apostles."

"So you're the original?"

Dave looked at her for a long moment, then caught the glint of humor in her blue eyes. He laughed. "Yeah, I guess I was."

Susan laughed too. She turned around, reaching her finger up and tracing the letters. Then she turned back to him. "So you wrote this?" she asked. He was so close to her, standing where he'd been when she'd hopped down from the rock.

"Yes," he said. "I carved it there with my pocket knife."

"In stone?" she said, surprised. "That must have taken a lot of work."

Dave shrugged, grinning. "I was here a lot."

Susan looked up at him, her eyes searching his, as if trying to find the source of such angst that he spent so much time at the beach alone.

Dave put his hands on the rock on either side of her head, lowering his head so his lips were within an inch of hers, staring into her eyes. "Don't look so worried," he said softly.

"I just…" she began, but his closeness overrode anything she would have said. "David…" she said, wanting to ask him to kiss her.

His lips touched hers before she could form her request. He kissed her gently at first, light, soft brushes on her lips, until her arms encircled his neck and her body pressed closer to his. His kiss intensified, making her moan softly in the back of her throat. His hands slid over her back, caressing her, his lips moving over hers expertly, making her feel weak instantly. She ran her hands through his hair, pulling his head down to hers, wanting the feelings he was causing in her. He clenched her waist, pulling her body closer.

Susan felt his tongue slide over her lips, parting them, and she was sure she was going to die. She'd never been kissed like this, even with Christian; she didn't know if it was the setting or the man, but she couldn't control her body. Her fingers clenched at his shoulders and back, her nails making marks she hadn't meant to make. His hands were caressing her back, her neck, sliding down past her waist.

When her hands moved under his shirt, her nails leaving a trail, he groaned aloud. He broke the kiss then, shaking his head as if telling himself no. Dave looked down at her, his eyes searching her face, as if wondering where she had come from.

In fact, he was wondering who the hell this girl really was. He had been just about ready to lose all control right there on the beach. He would have happily made love to her right there. This was not normal for him; he was always in control of himself, and he'd just about lost it. Jesus! He moved away from her, walking toward the ocean. Once at the water's edge he knelt down, gazing out. Susan stood watching him from the rock they'd been kissing against. She didn't understand his reaction. She didn't know if she'd done something wrong.

When Dave came back, he smiled at her but said nothing about what had happened. He took her hand and led her back to the car. Susan said nothing, not knowing how to ask him what she'd done wrong. A few blocks from the beach, Dave pulled into a gas station.

"Be right back," he said as he got out of the car.

Susan watched as he paid for his gas and then stuck the pump into the tank. He was leaning against the rear fender of the car, his arms crossed over his chest, when another man—a station attendant—approached him slowly.

"Dibbs?" the man said uncertainly.

Dave looked at the dark-haired man, his mind sensing familiarity but not coming up with a name to match the face.

"Yeah?" he said warily, always cautious, his thumb brushing the butt of his gun resting under his right arm in readiness.

"Dibbs, it's me, man—Jess," the man said, smiling.

Dave's mouth dropped open. "Jess?" he repeated incredulously. "Jesus, man!" He extended his hand. "How the hell have you been?"

Jess nodded, wiping his fingers on a dirty towel before shaking Dave's hand. "I've been okay," he said, his eyes roving over the midnight blue Charger. "Nice ride, man."

"Thanks," Dave said, his smile warm. "I rebuilt her myself."

"What year? Sixty-nine?"

"Seventy."

"Nice, nice…" Jess muttered as he slid his hand along the body of the car.

"Susan," Dave said as they got to the passenger door and Susan's open window. "This is Jess Jones. He was in the Apostles with me."

"It's very nice to meet you," Susan said, hiding well her surprise at meeting one of Dave's ex-members.

Jess looked back at her for a long minute. "You too, miss," he said, still looking like he hadn't totally understood her.

He walked to the front of the car as Dave went around to the driver's side and popped the hood. Once they had it up, Jess leaned over to Dave. "Nice shorty you got there," he said, grinning.

Dave looked back at him for a moment, then nodded, deciding it was easier than trying to explain to him that Susan wasn't his lady—well, not for now, she wasn't. It was too complicated. Jess checked out the 427 Hemi engine under the hood, appropriately impressed.

"Damn, you smoke 'em every time, don'tcha?"

"A lot," Dave said, grinning. He always enjoyed a chance to brag about his car.

They closed the hood. "So how've you been, Jess?" Dave asked as they walked back over to the driver's side of the car.

"Ah, I'm alright, Dibbs. Same shit, ya know?" Dave nodded. "I got married, and I got a kid." Jess shook his head. "Shit never was the same after you left. We all just went and did our own thing."

"Yeah?" Dave said vaguely, really not wanting to remind Jess that he was the one that had tried to take over the Apostles when Dave was out. He also didn't want to get into reminiscing about how Dave had pilfered half the gang's drug profits, the reason he'd "quit" the gang and joined FORS—mainly because the gang had wanted to kill him.

"Yeah, did you hear that Buddha and Sary got it?" Jess said.

Dave shook his head. "What happened?"

"They were banging with some gang over in Sidro. Another gang took 'em both out."

Dave grimaced, shaking his head. "Yeah, that shit'll get you killed."

"Tell me about it. Got my ass shot at one point. That's when I got out."

"Smart," Dave said, trying not to sound too condescending.

"Damn straight," Jess agreed. "So what're you doin' now?" he asked, nodding at the car behind Dave. "You must be pullin' down some serious Gs to be havin' a car like this. Right?"

"Nah, just workin', is all," Dave said, his answer purposely vague.

"Cool, cool," Jess said, his mind already wandering past the question. "Well, man, I better get back to it—the boss is a real pain in the ass. Stop by sometime, we'll go have a few beers at the Rathskeller. You remember that dump?"

Dave nodded. "Yeah, I remember."

"You take it easy, man," Jess said, clasping Dave's hand.

"You too, Jess, see ya," Dave said, getting into his car as Jess disconnected the pump.

As he drove away, Susan glanced over at him. Dave was looking in the rearview mirror, watching Jess wave. He stuck his arm out the window and raised his hand in a sort of a salute.

"He was in your gang?" Susan asked, still trying to assimilate that story.

"Yeah. He was the kid that thought he'd take over when I left."

"Really?" Susan asked, having noted that Jess didn't seem all that bright for a grown man.

Dave shrugged. "Guess he bought the act."

"The act?" Susan was lost again.

"Yeah," Dave said, picking his sunglasses up from the dashboard and putting them on. "I had an act that I used to make them all think I was harmless."

"And what was that act?"

Dave looked over at her. "Look and act as stoned as possible, as often as possible."

Susan stared back at him, surprised. "Were you ever stoned?"

"A number of times. But never near as far gone as they thought

I was. People tend to dismiss stonies, thinking they're too far out there to be any real threat."

"But you were," Susan said. "A threat."

"To anyone that tried to take what was mine."

Susan thought about that for a few minutes, then asked, "If you hadn't joined FORS, and you'd gone back to your gang, what would have happened to Jess and his bid for leadership?"

Dave didn't answer for a few moments, stopping at a red light and looking in the rearview again. He glanced over at her, his blue eyes hidden by the sunglasses, giving him a cold look. "I would have gone back and killed him for trying to take what was mine."

The tone of his voice told Susan he was serious, and also gave her a glimpse of the kind of gang leader he'd been. She'd fooled herself into thinking that he hadn't been dangerous then, but it sure sounded like he indeed had been. Possibly more so now—she wasn't sure, but she knew she was curious to find out.

A few minutes later, Dave pulled over to the side of the street. Susan turned to him, not sure why he had stopped. He pointed at a trailer park across the street.

"That's where I grew up," he said, staring straight ahead rather than where he was pointing. "Third trailer on the right."

Susan looked over at the trailer park. She had to admit that it did look pretty shabby, but she never would have said that to Dave. She could already see from the set of his jaw that he wasn't really comfortable with showing her this aspect of his life. She tried to see down to the trailer he'd indicated, but she couldn't see much. There was a run-down brown car parked there.

"Do your parents still live there?" she asked.

Dave shrugged. "Depends on whether they're in jail or not."

"Jail?"

Dave nodded. "I arrested them my first raid as a narc."

"Oh my lord," Susan said, unable to keep the shock out of her voice.

He glanced at her, his bitterness apparent. "I didn't know what we were hitting, but Spider did, and he tried to pull me off the raid team but didn't tell me who they were after. I insisted." He looked at his hands for a long moment, then back at her. "So I got the pleasure of arresting my own parents for running a meth lab."

Susan looked appropriately horrified. "David, that must have been awful," she said, reaching out to touch his arm.

He shrugged. "My old man actually fought, and ended up hitting me in the face. It took everything I had not to punch him back." He grinned. "Course, Spider took care of that. When he put my dad's cuffs on, he put them on nice and tight."

Susan smiled. "You and Spider are close, aren't you?"

Dave nodded. "He's always been my backup and basically my best friend." He started the car and drove off.

"You hungry?" he asked a few minutes later.

"Yes, I am, actually."

"You like Mexican food?"

"Yes, I guess so."

"Ever had Roberto's?" he asked, naming a Mexican fast food chain.

"I don't believe I have," she said, shaking her head.

He grinned. "Okay, then you need the experience. But first," he said as he took the freeway entrance, speeding up to pass a few cars, "I need to get out of this neighborhood."

He drove for a little while, finally taking an exit in Chula Vista. A few minutes later he pulled up in front of the taco stand. They ordered their food. To drink, Dave ordered a Corona and Susan asked for an iced tea. He grinned at the differences in their tastes.

They sat outside at one of the small stone tables. Dave took his sunglasses off as he ate.

"David?" Susan said.

"Yeah?"

"When you said you would have killed Jess for trying to take your place in the gang... you were serious, weren't you?"

He nodded as he took a long drink of his beer. He set the bottle down, placing his fingertip on the top of it. "You see, in a gang, it's life or death. There's no halfway."

"Yes, but... killing someone?"

"Susan, when you don't have anything to lose, you do what you think you have to do."

"Think?"

"Yeah," Dave said, sitting back in his chair, extending his legs out to the side, crossed at the ankles. "When you're in that mode, that way of thinking and acting, you can't see any other way to handle things."

"But you recognize now that you were wrong?"

Dave shrugged. "I know that if I hadn't left the gang, it would have come down to a fight with Jess, and I would have beaten him to death for control."

"But why?" Susan asked, struggling to understand him.

"There's no second best in the leadership of a gang, Susan. If you aren't the best fighter, the best wheel man, the best bullshitter, then you aren't their leader—they won't follow you. And most likely one of them will knife you in the back when you're not looking because they figure they can run the gang better than you."

"My lord," Susan said, aghast. "Why would anyone want to be in such a situation?"

Again Dave shrugged. "When your other option is to get killed by some gang because you're on your own, you choose to be part of a group that might protect you."

"But you started that gang, right?"

Dave nodded. "Yeah, there was a group of us that graduated high school at the same time. None of us were brain surgeon material, so we opted for hanging out together at a bar called the Rathskeller. It was a biker bar. One day I got into a discussion with some drunk biker about running drugs, and how easy it would be coming up the beach from Tijuana. He told me I needed to meet this other guy. I saw it as a way to make some cash, and after hooking up with the guy, formed the Apostles. We muled for a dealer and he paid us. We got the protection of a gang, and we got the profits of dealing, without hassle from the cops for selling stuff on street corners like other gangs did."

"Muled?" Susan asked.

"Yeah, it means that you basically smuggle the drugs in for the dealer."

"Like a mule hauls cargo."

"Right," Dave said, nodding.

Susan shook her head, seeing how easy it could be to fall into a pattern like that if you didn't have other options opened to you.

"But, David, you're intelligent—you could have gone to college or something."

Dave shrugged. "There was no money for that, and besides, most of the smarts I have now, I've acquired over the years."

Again Susan shook her head. "But you could have been killed…"

"Susan, I didn't much care in those days."

"I can't understand not caring about living or dying," she said, sounding very innocent.

"I didn't have much to live for at that point."

Susan looked back at him, surprised. "But your family…" she began, trailing off as she remembered what he'd told her about his mother and father.

"I hated them, they hated me."

"But didn't you have anyone you cared about and who cared about you?"

"No, I didn't. I grew up knowing that I was on my own."

"I can't imagine how hard that must have been for you," she said, reaching out to touch his hand. "I was always surrounded by family."

"Your parents?" Dave asked, having met Susan's mother briefly at the aborted wedding three years before.

"Well, actually, no. My father worked all the time and never had time for us, and my mother was dreadfully unhappy while married to him. She did her best, but she just didn't seem very warm. But my aunts and my uncle were always very nice to Liz and me. They always took us places and shared a lot of love with us."

"Liz is your sister, right?" Dave asked, vaguely remembering the younger girl at the wedding.

"Yes, she's three years younger than me."

"And a wild child, from what I remember," Dave said, grinning.

Susan laughed. "Oh, lord yes!"

Just then a lowrider went by, its bass-loaded music blasting. Dave glanced over Susan's shoulder, his eyes tracking the vehicle closely. She'd noticed him watching the street before that as well.

"You're on your guard all the time, aren't you?" she asked.

"I pretty much have to be."

Again, Susan couldn't fathom such a life. "When do you get any peace?"

Dave expelled his pent-up breath in a deep sigh. "At five a.m., on the ocean."

Susan smiled, nodding to show that she understood.

After a few more cars with blaring music rolled by, it became apparent that they couldn't have a decent conversation there. Once back in the car, Dave turned to her.

"Sorry about that," he said, grimacing. "The food's good, but the ambience is lousy."

Susan smiled. "It was fine, David. Don't worry."

"Tell you what," he said as he started the car. "What are you doing tonight?"

"Nothing really, once I put the children down for bed."

"Will Blue be there to keep an eye on things?"

"Yes, he said he'd be home tonight."

Dave nodded. "What time do the kids go down?"

"Seven."

"I'll pick you up at seven thirty."

"Okay…"

"I'm going to take you to a decent restaurant where the ambience isn't so…" He gestured around them at the street. "Colorful."

Susan smiled. "I'd like that."

"Then it's a date."

That night, Dave rang the bell at Joe's house feeling extremely strange. He realized this was way out of the ordinary, and it had just clicked in his head that Blue was likely to be there to see him pick Susan up when Christian opened the door. The Englishman's expression was puzzled at first, and then it obviously dawned on him that Dave was there for Susan. His light blue eyes narrowed.

"Dibbs," Christian said.

"Blue," Dave said, refusing to lower his eyes from the younger man.

Christian's lips curled into a sardonic grin as he stepped back, gesturing for Dave to enter. "You here for Susan?" he asked, his tone indicating it wasn't really a question.

Dave nodded, looking back at him.

"Grabbin' 'em a little young now, aren't ya?" Christian sneered.

"Last time I checked," Dave replied calmly, "Twenty-three's legal."

"Legal, yeah." Christian nodded. "Prudent, though… that's a whole other story."

"Well, I think I'll take my chances," Dave said, his tone still frustratingly calm.

"Your funeral," Christian said as he walked away.

Dave watched him go, wondering idly if the Englishman would find it necessary to tell Rick about him seeing Susan, just out of spite. He knew guys like Collins didn't like having what they considered theirs messed with. As far as Dave was concerned, Blue had given Susan away with both hands, so it was his problem if he didn't like her dating now.

"David," Susan said as she walked into the foyer, still putting on her earring so her head was turned to the side. "I didn't realize you were here already…" She trailed off as she looked up at him. She was stunned.

He was dressed in beige cotton slacks, a black shirt, and black suede shoes. He wore a dress belt that held his holstered weapon at the small of his back. There was no denying how handsome he was; she had never seen him looking so formal, and she was speechless for a moment.

"You look great," Dave said, smiling at her, the look in his eyes backing up that statement.

She wore a dress of cream, rose, and burgundy. The material was a sheer fabric that swirled around her knees as she moved. Her heels were burgundy as well. Her makeup had been applied with as much care as she could manage before she'd put the children down for bed. JT had exclaimed over how pretty she looked. Her hair flowed free, a silk curtain of honey-blond waves. In truth, she took Dave's breath away.

"Thank you," she replied shyly. "Shall we go?" she said, suddenly looking nervous as she glanced down the hall toward the living room. Apparently she was worried about what Christian would say.

Dave turned and opened the door for her. She walked out, and he followed her to the car. He opened the door for her, then went around and got in on the driver's side.

"Did Christian answer the door?" Susan asked.

Dave grinned. "Yep."

"Oh lord…" Susan said, biting her lower lip. "What did he say?"

"Let's just say he feels I'm dating below my age group," Dave said, an amused grin on his face.

"Oh, he's one to talk!" Susan gasped indignantly. "He dated a woman twice his age in England."

"Oh, really?" Dave asked as he started the car, still looking amused.

"Oh yes, really," Susan said, starting to grin too.

She was glad that whatever Christian had said apparently hadn't bothered Dave at all. She should have realized that Dave could hold his own with Christian's sharp tongue.

They were silent for a few minutes.

"I must say," Susan said, looking shy again, "you certainly look handsome tonight."

Dave smiled. "Thanks," he said, avoiding the urge to ask if she meant as opposed to any other night. He knew it wasn't what she'd meant, and didn't want to make her self-conscious about what she said to him.

"I don't recall ever seeing you dressed in... I mean..." Susan began, stammering when she realized that what she was trying to say might come out as condescending.

"So unlike a cop?"

"No," she said, laughing lightly. "Just so formally."

"Well," Dave said, rubbing his chin, "if you'd been paying attention at your wedding, I was dressed in a suit."

"Oh," Susan said, grimacing. "I guess I was a bit distracted that day."

"Just a bit," Dave said, smiling.

"Well, you look wonderful."

"Well, thanks," he said, grinning again.

"Can I ask where we're going to dinner?"

"The restaurant is called The Marine Room."

Susan was silent for a moment, not sure what to make of the name. Was it a restaurant for servicemen? That she knew of, Dave had never been in the military. She didn't want to ask and seem rude, so she kept silent.

They arrived at the restaurant a few minutes later. Susan realized then that they'd never left La Jolla. She was very surprised when he escorted her inside. Not only was the restaurant not a military servicemen's place, it was exceptionally lovely. The tables were elegantly clad in cream linen, the crystal and china place settings glowing, candles and flowers on each table. And the most incredible part of all was the setting. One entire wall of the restaurant was glass, looking out onto the ocean and the setting sun. Susan was speechless once again.

When she found her voice, she said, "David, it's lovely."

Dave had watched her for her reaction, realizing that the name of the restaurant had made her nervous. To her credit, she hadn't shown it, but Dave realized that with the way she'd been raised, something like the word *Marine* in a Navy town such as San Diego would not conjure up images of the sea, only thoughts of sailors and bars.

He placed his hand at the small of her back as they were escorted to a table next to the window. Dave sat with his back to the wall; Susan had noticed that he did that wherever they went. She commented on it.

"It's a cop thing," Dave said, shrugging. "I like to see what's going on around me, and not leave myself open from behind."

"Oh…" Susan said, looking around. "Even in a place like this?"

Dave smiled indulgently. "Even drug dealers eat in nice restaurants."

"Oh," she said, looking sufficiently subdued.

"Relax," he said. "I don't foresee any problems—I just like to be careful."

"Alright, then I'm in your hands," she said matter-of-factly.

"That you are."

They spent the next two hours dining, drinking wine, and talking. They talked about her childhood, about her education, and about her life growing up. Dave found that he liked her way of talking. She always put a positive spin on everything, explaining away things that normal people would harp on about. She didn't seem to let anything get her down. It was refreshing to hear about a happy childhood filled with love and everything she'd ever wanted. Susan was a surprising package; whereas she lacked the fire he thought he'd been searching for, she didn't in any way bore him, or make him feel like he needed to run off. He was constantly finding out interesting things about her ways of thinking, and she was so different than anyone he'd ever known before.

Dave thought all this as he watched her talk, smiling as she told a story about what one of the children had done that day. He found, too, that he enjoyed just listening to her. Her voice was almost melodic, and that combined with her accent, which was very much upper-class English, made her sound so different from anyone he'd ever talked to. He was used to ghetto speak, heavily accented slang, or streams of expletives.

After dinner, Dave drove down to the shore, where the waves rolled in against the rocks. He backed his car into a space looking out at the ocean. Grabbing a blanket, he laid it on the trunk. Susan was once again pleasantly surprised by his gentle ways. He lifted her by the waist to put her on the blanket, then gave her his black suede jacket when she shivered slightly. The evening was actually quite nice. There was no breeze, so it wasn't cold, just cool. The moon was full, so it was very bright. The stars twinkled in the sky and the waves crashed against the rocks only thirty or so feet away.

Dave ended up sitting with his back to the back window of the car, his knees pulled up to his chest, his arms draped over them. Susan eventually scooted between his legs, leaning back against him, her legs stretched out in front of her. He slid his arms around her waist. She leaned her head back on his shoulder as they talked. It was very comfortable. The warmth of his body kept her upper body warm, so she ended up laying his jacket over her legs. At one point during a comfortable lull in the conversation, she closed her eyes, turning her head toward his neck. She could smell the scent of his cologne, fresh and clean.

"What cologne do you wear?" she asked.

Dave grinned, enjoying the feeling of her against him, especially where her lips were at that moment. "It's called Cool Water."

Susan laughed lightly. "Well, that stands to reason, doesn't it?"

Dave chuckled. "I guess it would."

"David?" she said, sitting up and turning within the circle of his arms to look at him. "Today, at the beach…" she began, her eyes searching his. "Did I do something wrong?"

"No, you didn't do anything wrong," he said, reaching up to stroke her cheek.

"Then why did you walk away from me?"

Dave looked at her for a long moment, trying to decide how much he wanted to tell her, then figured, *What the hell?*

"Well, I've been with women for years, since I was about thirteen, so that's a good long time…" he began, his hand trailing down her cheek to her neck as he talked. "And I've gotten really good at controlling my responses." He slid his hand down to caress the place where her neck and shoulder met. "Today, I couldn't control myself with you."

Susan was taken aback, but at the same time she was trying to concentrate; the way he was touching her was making her feel quite warm.

"You…" she tried, her voice not coming out at first. "I mean, you couldn't?"

Dave grinned at her stammering, but didn't comment on it. "No."

"Do you think you'll ever kiss me again?" she asked as his hand moved back to her neck.

He nodded. "Probably."

His hand moved to the back of her neck, under her hair. Then he was pulling her to him, his lips taking possession of hers once again. The kiss was intense from the first second, and Susan gave in to it, sliding her hands up his chest. His other hand touched her waist, then grasped at it, pulling her closer. He extended his legs to either side of her body, and she lay against him, settling into a much more comfortable position to kiss him. Their lips never parted. They kissed for what seemed like hours on the trunk of his car.

Eventually, he got up, lifted her down, and drove to his house, holding her hand in the car all the way. Neither of them spoke. As she went into the bathroom to make some attempt to straighten herself up, Dave built a fire in the fireplace in his living room. They ended up lying on the floor in front of it, making love.

His hands moved over every inch of her skin almost reverently, caressing her, making her writhe and groan his name over and over again. It seemed like hours before his body finally slid into hers. She cried out immediately in her release, but Dave took his time, bringing her over and over again to that height. He finally took his release after making love to her for two hours. She lay in his arms and they kissed for a while, his hands constantly touching and caressing her, quickly bringing her to a fever pitch again. He made love to her again then, and so went most of the night.

At around three in the morning they moved to his bedroom because she was worried about his back, which he assured her was fine. He made love to her again in his bed, once again taking her to dizzying heights before allowing himself release. They were still breathing heavily when his phone rang. He glanced at it, then down at Susan, who lay in his arms.

"That's my undercover line," he said softly. "So don't say anything, okay?"

Susan nodded, looking subdued suddenly.

"Yeah?" Dave said into the phone. He listened for a long moment. "When's it coming in?" he asked, his voice sounding distinctly different than it normally did. "Shit, man, you want me to come up with 500K by tomorrow? You're fuckin' smokin too much of your own stuff." He listened again, staring up at the ceiling. "Yeah, yeah, I can do that," he said. "Maybe, I gotta make some connections." His eyes narrowed for a moment, then he nodded. "Yeah, I said I'll try, man. Okay?" He hung up a few moments later, then reached for his other phone.

"What was that?" Susan asked curiously.

"That was my short vacation coming to an end," Dave said, grinning down at her.

She lowered her head, kissing his chest. He moaned softly. "Hold that thought," he said, smiling down at her. He dialed his phone.

"Yeah, Spider?" he said. "Sorry to wake ya, man—tell Tammy I'm sorry—but I just got a call from Porter—it's a go for today at noon." He listened. "No, I don't want to take him down just yet, he says his source is coming with a hundred keys next month." He nodded. "Yeah, I'll be in at ten to get wired up." Another pause. "Okay, man, I'll see you then." He hung up after that, putting the phone down and turning to Susan, pulling her against him and kissing her deeply.

"You have to work," she said when their lips parted.

"Yeah," he said, kissing her again, "but I have some time."

"You do need some sleep," she said, gently chiding.

Dave glanced at the clock. "Yeah, about two hours' worth, so I got about three hours to kill."

"David!" she exclaimed, even as he moved her to her back, kissing her neck. "That's not enough sleep…" Her voice trailed off as she lost herself in the sensations he was causing. He made love to her again an hour later after driving her crazy, then slept for two and a half hours.

He kissed her as he left that morning. "I usually go out on these things for a couple of weeks," he said, kneeling next to the bed. "But I'll call you when I'm headed back in, okay?"

"Two weeks?" she exclaimed, surprised.

"Yeah…" he said, looking chagrined. "Sorry, hon."

Susan sighed, lying back on the bed and reaching out to touch his cheek. "I'll miss you," she said softly.

Dave smiled warmly at her then stood up, leaning down to kiss her softly on the lips. Then he was gone. Susan slept until noon, when he was meeting with his dealer, then took a shower and called a taxi to take her home. She felt totally different now. She felt so happy she was sure everyone would see it, but she didn't care.

Christian intercepted her at the front door when she walked in.

"You fucked him?" he asked without prelude, incredulous.

Susan looked back at him for a long moment. "You fucking Stevie O'Neil?"

Christian narrowed his eyes at her. "It's a revenge fuck?"

Susan expelled her breath in an annoyed sigh, shaking her head. "No, Christian—that's your style, not mine." Without another word she moved past him and went to her room.

Christian watched her go, a stunned look on his face. Then he started to grin. He chuckled to himself. Rick Debenshire would kill Dave if he found out. He had to hand it to Dave, though—the man did know how to operate.

CHAPTER 7

Donovan opened the sliding glass door leading out to the deck at Joe and Randy's house. Joe was sitting in one of the Adirondack chairs, a drink in hand, as he watched his kids playing on the beach. He glanced up when he heard the door open.

"Hey, Donovan," he said, his accent thicker because he'd been drinking.

Donovan glanced down at the beach and noticed, to his relief, that Susan was there to watch the children.

"Hey, Joe," he said casually.

Erin was standing right next to him, but out of Joe's line of sight. It was obvious to Donovan that she felt weird about the new level of their relationship. She was afraid everyone would think she was trying to take Jeanie's place.

"Joe," Donovan said, taking Erin's hand and tugging her forward, "this is Erin."

Joe looked up at her, his light blue eyes hidden by sunglasses. "Nice to meet you."

"You too, sir," Erin said respectfully.

Joe immediately made a face. "It's Joe—no one calls me sir, unless they're in trouble."

Erin bit her lip, but grinned too.

"So what are you drinking?" Donovan asked, noting that it wasn't the brand of tequila Joe usually drank.

"Tequila Sunrise," Joe said, holding the glass up in a silent toast and draining it.

"I think I'll get one," Donovan said. "You want another?"

"Sounds like a great plan," Joe said, his eyes going out over the ocean.

Donovan leaned down to Erin. "Do you want anything?"

She shook her head, smiling at him.

Donovan went back into the house, and Erin stood there, feeling really out of place.

"So," Joe said after a long silence. "You work at the department too?"

"Yes, sir—um, Joe. I'm in the secretarial pool."

Joe smiled at her correction, then nodded. "Some good secretaries in that pool."

Erin laughed softly. "I heard you met your wife there."

"Well, she was my secretary, but she was never in the pool."

"Oh?" Erin said. "She's lucky. I hate being so transient."

"Why's that?"

Erin shrugged. "I would rather be great at one job than mediocre at a lot of them."

Joe looked thoughtful for a minute, then nodded. "That's a good point. Have you applied for any of the permanent positions in the department?"

Erin shook her head. "I've only been here a few months—I figured I'd learn the ropes first."

Again Joe nodded. "Come see me when I get back in the office. I might be able to help you out."

"Really?" Erin said, surprised. "Thanks."

"No problem," Joe said as he glanced up at her again. "So, you dating Donovan?"

"Umm…" Erin stammered, not sure how to answer. Joe waited. "Well, sort of."

"Sort of?"

"Well, we're more friends than anything else," she explained, feeling really foolish.

Joe looked at her for a long moment, then nodded slowly. "My wife tells me you're in love with him."

Erin just stared back at him, unsure what to say. Just then, Donovan walked back outside and handed Joe his drink.

"Cheers," Joe said, taking a sip. "Gad!"

"What?" Donovan asked.

Joe made a face. "There's a helluva lot of orange juice in here."

Donovan chuckled. "Sinclair, it's supposed to have orange juice in it."

"Yeah, but this much?" Joe said, looking at Donovan suspiciously.

"Three parts OJ, one part tequila."

Joe looked at him for a full minute, then shook his head. "You're off the bartender list. I need to go fix this." He got up out of his chair and walked past them into the house.

Donovan grinned down at Erin. "So what were you two talking about?"

"Oh, nothing," Erin said, trying to sound casual.

Donovan looked at her for a long moment, then shook his head, knowing she wasn't telling him the truth but willing to let this one go.

When Joe came back out they talked about inconsequential things. A little while later Donovan and Erin left. Everyone had been over to see Joe, noting that he was drinking heavily but not saying anything, realizing that this was how Joe Sinclair dealt with serious stress in his life.

Rick walked out onto the deck two hours later. "Hey," he said to Joe.

"Hey," Joe answered, not even looking up.

"How's it goin'?"

"It's goin'."

Rick nodded, his eyes scanning the horizon.

"Midnight send ya?" Joe asked.

Rick grinned. "No, I came all on my own. Go figure, huh?"

"Uh-huh," Joe replied, giving his best friend a cynical look.

Rick reached down, plucking Joe's drink out of his hand and taking a sip.

"Damn, Joe, that's almost pure tequila!" he said, wincing.

"Yeah, so?" Joe sounded highly unconcerned.

"So," Rick said, grinning, "why not just drink shots?"

Joe looked thoughtfully at his glass, then shrugged. "I figured this was like breakfast."

Rick laughed, looking at his watch. "It's two o'clock, man."

"Shit," Joe said, sounding disgruntled. "Time to switch to straight tequila."

Rick laughed again and went inside, grabbing the bottle of tequila and two glasses. "Where's Randy?" he asked as he poured them both shots.

"School," Joe said, shrugging. "No point in her education going to shit, right?"

"True," Rick said as he held up his glass. Joe lifted his as well and they both drank.

"So," Joe said, giving his friend the critical eye, "you recovered?"

Rick shrugged. "I'm sore as hell," he said as he poured two more shots. "But I'll live."

"Told ya not to step in front of bullets," Joe said, and raising their glasses once more, they drank again.

The afternoon proceeded in much the same manner. Midnight stopped by Joe's house at six o'clock, coming out onto the deck where both men still sat as the sun went down.

"I see," she said, giving her husband and best friend a dirty look. "Drinking without me, are you?"

"Sorry, love," Rick said, sounding very English and fairly drunk as well. He patted the spot next to him on the lounge chair. "Come join us."

"Do I get my own shot glass?" Midnight asked.

"Nah," Rick said, grinning. "You gotta share mine."

"You have germs, Debenshire," Midnight said, and laughed at the face he made.

He winked. "Nothing you haven't had before, love."

The three of them proceeded to have a few drinks, and Randy found them an hour later, laughing and joking.

"What's going on out here?" she asked.

"Hey, babe," Joe said, reaching up to grab her hand.

"Hey, handsome," Randy said as he pulled her down on his lap, kissing her lips softly. She grinned. "Oh, we've had a few, haven't we?"

"Oh yeah," he said, grinning unrepentantly. "Wanna join us?"

"I wish I could, but I have a test tonight. I just wanted to come home and check on you and the kids."

"We're fine," Joe said, indicating himself, Midnight, and Rick.

"I meant our kids, Joe," Randy said, laughing. "Not you kids."

Midnight and Rick laughed then too. Randy found herself glad that Rick and Midnight had come to Joe's rescue. She'd heard from Donovan earlier in the day that he was drinking heavily, and had put in a call to Midnight about it. Joe had been insistent on Randy going to class, so she knew she couldn't come running home to keep an eye on him. Midnight had contacted Rick to see if he could free himself up to go hang out with Joe; Rick had been more than happy to do so. It paid to have such a good circle of friends.

That night, Randy walked into her and Joe's bedroom to find her husband sitting on the bed, on the phone. She glanced at the clock; it was ten. She went into the bathroom to wash off her makeup and brush out her hair, and when she came back into the bedroom he was off the phone.

"Who was that, this late at night?" she asked.

"Robert."

Randy looked at him for a long moment. "Why was Robert calling?"

"Because I left a message for him to call me first thing in the morning England time."

"Why?" Randy knew she wasn't going to like his answer.

Joe stared at her, then leaned his head back against the wall, looking up at the ceiling. "Because I wanted to make some changes in my will," he said, as if saying it so simply would lessen the impact.

"Joe..." Randy began.

"Randy, this is important, okay?"

"Why? Why is it important, Joe? You're not going to die, damnit. You're going to be fine—everything is going to be fine."

"And if it's not?" he asked, his voice holding a tremor.

"Then we'll deal with it then, Joe. Please..." she said, her voice becoming a bit shaky.

"I left Donovan, Darrell, and Christian a million each," he said. "You and the kids get the house, the estate, and the remainder of everything else. I've left—"

"Joe, stop!" Randy held up her hands in defense against what he was saying. "I don't want to hear this. You're not going to die—this isn't important."

"It is, Randy," Joe said, his voice softening. "I need to know that the people I care about the most will be taken care of."

Randy closed her eyes for a long moment, swallowing convulsively as she tried to gain control over her emotions. "Please don't do this…" she said quietly.

"Randy, there's more," Joe said, even as she held up her hands in a halting gesture. "You need to hear it all."

Randy sat down on the bed, her eyes on him, begging him not to continue, but he did.

"If they diagnose me with lung cancer, I'm not doing any treatment." Randy's sharp intake of breath was audible, but Joe continued, as if driven to say everything he needed to before she stopped him. "That means no radiation, no chemotherapy, none of that shit. We both know that lung cancer is a death sentence, and I have no intention of trying to put off the inevitable."

"Joe, it doesn't mean that, it—"

"Yes, it does."

"But Joe…" Randy said, shaking her head.

"Randy, I won't have the last memory my kids or you have of me as this ghost of what I used to be. I won't do that," Joe said, his voice softening.

He saw suddenly that she was shaking, and felt a stab of guilt for dumping all of this on her. He'd been mulling it over all day, while drinking, and wanted it settled and out of the way. He had always known that if he ever got some deadly disease like cancer, he would give in and let it take him. He'd seen what fighting the ravages of cancer got the victim, and it was exactly nothing. But now, he realized that Randy hadn't been thinking about it all day like he had, and she hadn't been prepared for all that he'd said.

Reaching out, he pulled her into his arms, holding her close. "I'm sorry," he whispered against her hair.

Randy allowed herself a few minutes of weakness then, clinging to him as she cried. His words had made the possibility of lung cancer more real, and it scared her. Her life would never be the same if she lost him, and she hadn't even wanted to think about what would happen. But Joe had just shown her graphically what that would be, and it made her sick to her stomach.

After a while she calmed down again, regaining her composure. She looked up at him, searching his eyes; she could see the chagrin in them.

"I love you," she said softly. "We're going to get through this."

Joe closed his eyes for a moment, then nodded.

He held her extra close all night, apologizing with his nearness in a way he couldn't in words.

The addendum to the original slanderous article was printed in the following day's *San Diego Tribune*:

True Love in the Face of Trouble

Lieutenant Rick Debenshire was shot this week in a gun fight with a man intent on killing his wife, Chief Midnight Chevalier-Debenshire. The man's name, Julio Martinez, was not unfamiliar to the Debenshires; he is the man responsible for

227

the car bomb that almost ended the life of Midnight Chevalier.

That there was a gunfight in San Diego is not newsworthy. The fact that a police officer was shot in the line of duty is also not the focus of this article. The fact that the bullet that struck Richard Debenshire was intended for his wife is what has this reporter reevaluating his previous article pertaining to Chief Midnight Chevalier and her department.

In an effort to clarify my previous writing regarding an incongruous letter sent to the city council, I went to the hospital the night Richard Debenshire was shot. I had a chance to talk to the lieutenant. I also had a rare opportunity to talk to Chief Chevalier-Debenshire herself (Chief Chevalier rarely, if ever, gives personal interviews).

Chief Chevalier was quite articulate in her response to the assertions in the letter. She indicated that her time in the department as well as her record speak for themselves. In a fashion befitting the law degree she holds, Chief Chevalier was succinct in her refusal to enter a battle of hearsay with an unknown attacker. Her husband, still sitting in the hospital bed he was put in after surgery to remove the bullet that hit him, supported her wholeheartedly.

In this reporter's opinion, the letter writer is no more than a disgruntled employee. The city council has stated that they intend nothing more than a cursory

investigation of the allegations, since no
real examples or facts were presented.

Further, this reporter would like to comment that the Debenshire love affair is
alive and well, and it certainly made an
impression on this ordinarily staunch
cynic of "love."

Rick read the article that morning, and got a call from Midnight just as he was picking up the phone to call her. They laughed over the last paragraph, saying the reporter definitely needed to get out more. There was a lot of relief that day in the face of the stress over Joe's situation.

Work on the departmental inventory began the following day. The team consisted of Rhiannon, Christian, Erin, Stevie, Kyle, and two other women from the secretarial pool who spent a great deal of time drooling over Christian, which Stevie found endlessly amusing. They split into pairs, one peace officer with one non-sworn person. Kyle worked with every group. Christian grabbed Erin, because at least she didn't seem like a panting puppy.

The lists had been run off, so each pair got a stack of them, one list for each unit they were to inventory. Erin and Christian headed off. As they worked, Christian asked her about Donovan.

"You with him now?" he asked as he checked off two more items she showed him from the equipment closet they were working through.

Erin looked at him for a long moment, trying to determine if he was asking to be malicious or if he was just curious. Finally she shrugged. "He's in love with someone else, so I'm pretty temporary."

"I know," Christian said. "Jeanie is a friend of mine."

"Oh," Erin said, thinking she'd just screwed up nicely.

Christian grinned. "Don't worry. I'm pretty pissed at Jeanie for this dumb-shit move too."

"Oh, good," Erin said, grinning in relief. "I'm friends with her too, but I just don't get why she did this."

Christian shrugged. "Someone told her once that she needed to be independent, and she's taking it way too far." He pinned her with a look. "He's fucked up, isn't he?"

Erin bit her lip, not wanting to cause any problems. "He's better now."

Christian narrowed his eyes at her, as if looking for deception, then nodded, and they continued their inventory.

The following day, Joe found himself driving over to the range with Stevie O'Neil. He'd just come back that day, tired of sitting at home waiting for the test results. As part of her task, Stevie was to inventory the firearms. That meant talking to Joe Sinclair, who was the current acting rangemaster for the department, since the last rangemaster had retired two months before. They were both fairly quiet, Joe because he was severely hungover from his drinking binge of the last few days, and Stevie because she wasn't sure what to say to him.

When they reached the range, Joe was surprisingly attuned to what Stevie was looking for. He printed out a list of weapons and who they'd been issued to. He then showed her all of the weapons kept at the range for practice. She was further impressed when he was able to produce documentation to show guns that were currently with the gunsmith for repair, as well as returns to Glock for replacement. Stevie made a comment about how organized he was.

Joe grinned. "You get audited a few times, and get yer ass chewed out by the chief for not being able to locate a gun, and you learn to document."

Stevie laughed. "I don't think Chief Chevalier would ever chew you out."

"Like hell she wouldn't," Joe said, rolling his eyes. "She does so rather frequently."

"Uh-huh," Stevie said, sounding unconvinced.

After that, things were more relaxed. On the way back to the office, they'd stopped at a light that had just changed red when a white sedan ran through it. Joe's eyes tracked the car, and once it had cleared the intersection he proceeded ahead.

"He just ran a red," Stevie commented.

Joe glanced to the right, watching the car go, then shrugged. "I've been off patrol for so long I don't even care anymore."

"I guess I'm still pretty fresh on it," Stevie said. "Hell, at this point, I'm just glad I have a job."

"Training and development is a good place to be."

"Oh, I know," Stevie assured him. "I'm just grateful not to be in jail. If Midnight had seen fit to make me a meter maid I would have been perfectly happy."

Joe laughed, shaking his head. "Nah, Midnight doesn't waste talent like that."

"Talent?"

"Yeah," Joe said, glancing over at her. "Stevie, you took down a dealer that even Dave hadn't been able to get to—that's talent."

"Dave made that bust, not me," Stevie objected.

"You made the case—Dave just helped you deliver it."

Stevie was silent for a few minutes, absorbing the fact that she was being given credit for Tiempo's arrest. She sighed heavily. "I just hope I don't let her down," she said, expressing her deepest fear.

Joe looked over at her again as they entered the department parking lot. His light blue eyes, so much like Christian's, narrowed, and then he shook his head. "You won't."

"How do you know?"

Joe shrugged. "Midnight doesn't make mistakes when she assigns people. She knows what she's doing."

"I hope so," Stevie said. Even so, her spirit was buoyed by Joe's words.

She talked to Christian about it that night after they'd worked the chat room some more. Working on the case usually meant chatting and recording all the conversations they thought would lead to something, then running down the ISP addresses. Most nights afterward, they'd end up in bed together, either his or hers, depending on whose house they'd been working at. That's where many of their conversations took place, while their bodies were still intertwined.

"So, Joe thinks you can do this," Christian said, his hand still caressing her waist.

Stevie lay next to him, propped up on one elbow on her side, her hand on his chest. "Yeah."

"And that means what?" he asked, one jet black eyebrow lifted sardonically.

Stevie made a disgusted sound in her throat, moving to lie on her back. "Jesus, Collins," she said, as if not believing he could be so dumb.

Christian turned onto his side. "What?" he asked as he grinned down at her, sounding very English.

Stevie pinned him with a look. "Your cousin is the best of the best in terms of investigations. If Joe Sinclair thinks I can handle this assignment then he's probably right."

"You didn't believe you could handle it?" Christian asked, surprised at this less confident side of her, and oddly pleased that she was sharing it with him.

Stevie shrugged. "I don't know," she said, looking back at him. "I guess I figured the Tiempo thing was revenge driven, that maybe I wouldn't be as effective in a real case situation, you know?"

Christian nodded. "So, Joe saying that he believed you could handle it makes you more likely to believe it?"

"Yeah." Stevie looked chagrined. "It's stupid, I know."

Christian didn't say anything for a long moment, then grinned, leaning down to kiss her neck. "Not stupid, just kind of a lot of hero worship."

Stevie had told him about how she had basically worshiped Joe and Midnight when she was growing up. He had found it amusing, but hadn't been able to say much, since he thought Midnight was the ideal woman. He also admired his cousin more than he'd ever admit even to himself.

"I'm headed out of town at the beginning of next week," he said.

"Oh yeah? Where?"

"San Francisco. SFPD wants me to install the inventory system."

"Ah," Stevie said, nodding. "So how long will you be gone?"

"'Bout two weeks." He kissed her shoulder. "Will you miss me?" he asked, grinning devilishly.

"Nope," she said, turning over on her side and putting her back to him. He caught the grin on her lips as she did.

He moved closer to her, pulling her back against him at the same time. He put his lips to her neck, kissing her skin, then nipped at her earlobe. "Yes, you will."

"Like hell—" she began, but his body pressing against hers and his fingers sliding over her skin caused her to gasp. God! It was absolutely criminal, how easily this man could excite her.

"You'll miss me," he said again as his body slid inside hers, his hands guiding her hips to move with him.

Stevie didn't answer him, groaning instead. Yes, she would miss him, but she'd be damned if she'd give him the satisfaction of hearing her say that.

The following day, when Joe Sinclair walked through the department it was with a sense of unreality. He went to the elevators and took one to the top floor, then headed to Midnight's office. The expected crowd was there. He'd had his assistant call everyone in so he could tell them all at the same time. He'd gotten the results of his test.

As he walked into Midnight's office, he could see that she was worried. She stood in front of Rick; his hands were on her shoulders. Kyle leaned against the wall looking very serious. Spider was sitting

234

at the round table with Kana and Tiny. Donovan was there too, so Randy hadn't had a chance to call him. Christian was leaning against the front of Midnight's desk, his legs crossed at the ankles, his arms over his chest. It was obvious to Joe that the younger man was worried, but to anyone that didn't know him well, they'd think he was unconcerned. The only core member that wasn't there was Dave Dibbins, because he was still out on undercover work.

Joe kicked the door closed. He looked around at all his friends, then shook his head.

"Jesus, it's not a bloody wake, people—lighten up," he said, his voice a deep growl.

Midnight canted her head to the side. "Joe…" she said, trailing off as he started to grin. "It was negative?" she breathed, almost afraid to say it out loud, because it might make her wake up if she was dreaming.

"It was negative," Joe affirmed.

The group sighed together, then all moved to Joe to shake his hand. Joe caught Christian's nod and grinned to himself. *Still playing it cool*, he thought. The group gave way as Midnight walked over to Joe, reaching up to hug him.

"Thank God," she whispered, her face buried against his shirt.

"I did," Joe murmured.

She laughed softly, then stepped back to look up at him. "So what is it anyway?"

Joe shrugged. "Some infection—that's why I've had the cough. Doctor said some antibiotics and some rest and I'll be just fine."

"Since when do you rest?" Rick asked.

"You're one to talk, Debenshire," Donovan put in, making the group laugh.

"Shut up, Curtis," Rick said, grinning all the while.

Everyone was so happy about the results, and of course the good news spread through the office like wildfire. Spider even sent Dave a page to tell him everything was okay, using Joe's radio call number and giving a 10-8, meaning Joe was back on duty.

When Dave got the page, he was sitting on the deck of his latest target's beach house. The kid was scum; Dave could barely stand to be around him. He was a Mexican who had come up the hard way. He had a gang that ran drugs for him, and he was renowned for having killed a number of people on his way up. They called him El Loco, "The Crazy One." He liked to entertain, and he liked to show off how much money and power he had.

He was the man that Dave had had a deal with. They'd done their business, but Dave wasn't ready to take him down just yet. He was waiting for the big guy. El Loco had a supplier that got him high-grade methamphetamine, and Dave wanted to take down the source too. He knew he wouldn't lose El Loco in the bargain, because the kid was too sure of himself to ever run. So Dave was biding his time.

Unfortunately, biding his time meant playing nice with the guy, and to that end he was at a party El Loco was having for Cinco de Mayo. The party had been going on for a week already. Dave fell into his usual stoned routine to appear less conspicuous. He'd found early on in his life that the more stoned you seemed, the less people noticed you. That's when they talked, and sometimes they talked about things he wanted to know.

Sitting on the deck, a bottle of beer in hand, shades in place,

Dave looked like the casual drug dealer he played. His long legs were stretched out in front of him as he slumped low in the chair, wearing faded jeans and a long Hawaiian shirt. With the scruff of a three-day beard, he looked like a bum. The gold Celtic cross around his neck was the only jewelry he wore.

"Hey, amigo," Loco said from behind him.

"Yeah, man?" Dave said, slurring his voice slightly.

"You see that pretty one down there?" Loco said, squatting down next to Dave's chair.

Dave looked in the direction he was pointing. "Which one, man?"

"That one, the blond."

After a few moments, Dave nodded.

"I'm gonna tap that ass," Loco said lasciviously.

"She looks like a kid, man," Dave said, feeling his stomach turn over.

"Hey, if they're old enough to open up, they're old enough to say ahhhh." Loco laughed at his own humor.

Dave grinned, all the while thinking, *I don't think so, asshole.* He made a mental note to keep an eye on Loco. The girl did look pretty young, maybe around thirteen or fourteen. Fortunately, a little while later she left the beach before Loco got a chance to get near her. It reminded Dave of why he was in this business—to take people like Loco off the street, where they did more than sell drugs.

"Where'd she go?" Loco all but whined when he realized the girl had disappeared.

Dave shrugged, unconcerned. "Musta left."

"Shit," Loco said, pouting. "Well, fuck it. Come on in the house, man. We're gonna do some hits."

Dave looked like he was thinking about it for a minute, then shook his head, holding up his beer. "Still comin' down off a jag."

"Come on, man, this is good shit," Loco cajoled.

"Nah, I'm cool. I'm already pretty wasted."

Loco shrugged. "No prob, more for me." He laughed and walked into the house. Dave sat watching the waves, his mind focused on what was being said around him. He picked up comments about Loco's latest hit; Dave waited for the name, but no one seemed to know who he was going to take out.

A few hours later, he had gone to stand at the deck after getting another beer. It seemed like he'd had at least a case by then, but in truth he'd only drunk about three total. He knew how to make it look like more. The breeze was coming up, and Dave shivered. He walked through the house and out to his car, then leaned through the open window and pulled out his leather jacket.

"Heya," a female voice said from behind him.

He turned around and recognized the woman as one of Loco's girlfriends.

"Hey," he replied coolly.

"What ya doin' out here?" she asked, her gum snapping as she chewed incessantly. She'd probably been a pretty girl at one point, with dark hair and dark eyes and a decent figure, but she'd been on one too many crystal jags and the drug had ravaged her features.

Dave held up his jacket. "I was cold."

She moved closer, and Dave found himself backed up against his own car, his hands held up and out to his sides. He had no intention of touching her; she was with Loco, and he didn't need the dealer on him about making time with his lady.

"I could keep you warm," she breathed into his face, her hands at his waist.

Dave did his best to hold his breath; she smelled of mint gum, pot smoke, and beer.

"Hey, Juana, thanks," he said, his tone anything but a come-on. "But I like my ass without any holes in it, and I think Loco would bust a cap in it if I took up with you."

Juana smiled, obviously liking that Dave was afraid of her boyfriend and thinking she had the upper hand here.

"He doesn't have to know," she said, her hand sliding down between them, moving to unzip his jeans.

He pushed her back gently. "No way."

"What are you? Gay or somethin'?" she sneered.

"Nah," he said, flipping his jacket over his shoulder. "Just smart." With that he walked away, leaving her standing there.

When he got back to the deck, he pulled on his jacket. He was immediately assailed with the scent of jasmine. His heart tripped a beat as his mind took him right back to the beach a week before with Susan. He closed his eyes for a moment, remembering the way she'd looked up at him, the way her hand had felt moving up his chest, the feel of her hair in his hands, the taste of her lips on his. He felt his entire body tighten in longing. He was so lost in his thoughts he didn't hear Loco talking to him.

He did feel the fist that slammed into his jaw though. Dave

found himself lying on the ground, looking up at Loco, who danced around in a show of readiness.

"Get up, puto!" Loco yelled.

"What the?" Dave replied, his voice barely coherent. "Wah, man?" he muttered, shaking his head and crawling to his knees.

"You fucked with my bitch."

"Huh?" Dave realized exactly what had happened; Juana had gone to Loco and lied to him because Dave had turned her down. He climbed to his feet, staggering uncertainly.

"Look at him, man," another guy said. "He's fucked up—he couldn't have fucked her."

"Fucked who?" Dave asked blearily, playing the stoned-guy part to the hilt.

"Me, you pig!" Juana spat.

Dave stared at her as if he was having trouble focusing. "When?"

"Earlier, estupido!" Juana said, seeing that people were looking at her now.

"I was here?" Dave asked, for all intents and purposes clueless.

"Yeah, man, you were here," Loco said, already sounding calmer. He could see that Dave was too loaded to have had any kind of sex with Juana.

"Oh shit, man, okay," Dave said, his stance wavering, and then he fell forward as if he were passing out. One of the guys nearby caught him, thankfully before he hit the deck. But better the wooden planks hit him than Loco decide to shoot him. Dave knew it would blow his whole cover if he had to shoot the dumb kid. He heard Loco make a sound of exasperation, and then to his relief he told Juana to go play her stupid games with someone else's head. Dave was moved to a chair and left there to wake up on his own.

He sat there for a while, but it was obvious everyone had gone back into the house. Slowly he sat up, reaching up to touch his lip. Predictably it was bleeding; Loco wore a lot of rings. He sat back, resting his head on the back of the chair, his jacket gathered around his face. Turning his head, he could smell Susan's perfume again.

"Shit," he said, sitting up.

After a few minutes he got up and went out to his car. He got in, started the engine with a roar, and threw it into gear, driving off in a storm of gravel and dust. Speeding down the highway, he changed the radio station a few times, finally pushing in a tape. It was Staind's latest, and the song that came on, "It's Been Awhile," made him reach over and turn the volume up. The Bose speakers he had installed rose to the occasion, blaring out at top volume without a bit of distortion. He sang along with the words. The lyrics bemoaned not having a normal life, and Dave felt the words in his very being at that moment in time.

He knew his getting too deeply involved with Susan could be dangerous. Hell, he'd lost all sense of time and place when he'd simply smelled her perfume. It was crazy! It wasn't like he was a kid experiencing sex for the first time. He'd been with hundreds of women—why was she so different? He didn't know, but he did know that she was in his head, and he needed to get her out while he was working.

Dave spent the next few hours driving and listening to music. Finally he went back to the apartment he used when he was undercover. He dropped down on the bed and lay there in the dark, his eyes wide open. Nothing was working; he couldn't get her out of his head.

"Damnit," he growled.

Rolling over, he reached for his cell phone, knowing it was crazy but not caring at that point. He dialed Susan's number, her own line at Joe's. It rang a couple of times. Dave looked at the clock on the shabby nightstand; it was 11:30 p.m. He let it ring a couple more times, then decided it was a bad idea. As he went to press the END button, he heard her answer.

"Hello?" she said, her voice quiet and sleepy.

Dave was silent for a moment, not sure if he should just hang up instead. Eventually, he said, "Susan, it's me."

"David?" she asked, instantly sounding worried.

"Yeah," he said hesitantly.

"Is everything alright?"

"Yeah, everything's okay," he said softly.

"Thank goodness," Susan replied. She sounded so young and so innocent.

She is young, you idiot, he told himself, thinking again that he had been stupid to call her.

"David?" Susan asked when he didn't speak again.

"I'm here."

"Are you sure you're alright?"

"Yeah…" he said, trailing off. "I just…" he started, then hesitated again, questioning the intelligence in telling her what he was thinking.

"Just what, David?" Susan asked softly.

"I just wanted to hear your voice," he said. He felt like an idiot, but it was true. It had been almost a week since he'd left, and he found that he missed her.

Susan smiled, her heart soaring. He had a way of putting things that made her feel so special.

"I can't really talk right now," he said, suddenly feeling like he was indeed crazy for having called her from the apartment, and on his cell phone no less. Cell phones could be traced; he knew that.

"Okay," Susan said, trying to tamp down on her disappointment. She knew that what Dave did for a living was dangerous, and that he had to be careful. She had missed him though, more than she'd realized she would.

"I'll talk to you in a week or so when I get back," he said, sounding vague all of a sudden.

"Alright," Susan answered automatically, realizing he suddenly sounded like Christian did when he called from his business trips. The thought made her feel disappointed. Was she being brushed off so quickly?

"Bye," Dave said briskly.

"Goodbye, David," Susan said solemnly. A second later he broke the connection.

Susan lay awake the rest of the night, not sure what she had done wrong. She fought off tears, as well as thoughts of being used. Just because he hadn't been able to talk just then, didn't mean that he didn't want to see her again. That was just her assumption. She told herself that over and over again, finally falling asleep before dawn, a half hour before her alarm went off.

Kyle and Rhiannon were working together on the inventory and the information they were getting back. They had spent hours poring over reports, trying to determine how best to proceed. It took a few very long days. One day they worked until 6:30, when Kyle stood up and stretched, looking at his watch.

"It's getting late—let's call it a day," he said.

Rhiannon looked up at the clock, surprise clear on her face. She hadn't realized it was that late. She nodded, standing up to stretch as well. As she did, she felt a muscle spasm in her shoulder, and she gasped at the sharp pain.

"You okay?" Kyle asked.

"Yeah," Rhiannon said, reaching up to rub her shoulder. "I injured it pretty bad in the accident back then."

Kyle nodded. "And here I am, overworking you."

"Kyle, stop. I'm fine."

"Well," he said, looking thoughtful. "I'm without children tonight—can I take you to dinner?"

Rhiannon looked at him for a long moment. Then she shrugged. "Sounds like a good idea," she said, smiling.

He grinned. "Good."

They went to dinner at a local fish restaurant, Anthony's. The sun was going down as they sat down at their table. Since the restaurant overlooked the bay, it was a very pretty sight. That night they talked about a lot of topics, debating some and just discussing others. Kyle told her about his son Nick's current stream of complaints. He hated California, he hated his new school, he hated his father.

"Is he still upset about losing his mother?" Rhiannon asked gently.

Kyle nodded. "That's part of it."

"What's the other part?" she asked, picking up her glass of wine and taking a sip.

"He had a little racket going back in New York—he was starting to run numbers for his uncle."

"Oh boy," Rhiannon said, remembering what Kyle had told her about Barbara's family being connected.

"Yeah, he was in for making some money," Kyle said grimly. "And now he's added that to the list of charges on my head."

Rhiannon shook her head. "Will he get used to San Diego eventually, do you think?"

Kyle shook his head miserably. "I don't know." He shrugged. "If nothing else, he can move back to New York when he's eighteen, if that's what he wants."

"But you don't want that," Rhiannon pointed out wisely.

"No. But I don't think I'm going to get a choice in the matter."

Rhiannon reached across the table, touching his hand. "Kyle, all you can do is be there for him. You can't make him hear you."

Kyle nodded, looking into her eyes. "I know, I just—" he began, but stopped as emotion threatened to overflow for a moment. He swallowed a few times against the lump in his throat. "I just don't want to lose him too."

"You won't," Rhiannon said, with more assurance in her voice than he'd heard in a long time from anyone. It warmed him somehow.

They moved on to other topics, and eventually left the restaurant. He drove her back to the department parking lot. Again there was the hesitation, neither of them sure what to say.

"Thank you, I had a nice time," she said, feeling like she sounded dumb.

Kyle grinned at the canned phrase. "I bet you say that to all the boys."

"Oh yeah, all the time," Rhiannon said airily, and laughed.

"That's what I figured," he said, grinning still.

His face grew serious a moment later as he reached out, touching her cheek, then slid his hand behind her neck to pull her to him. His lips covered hers in a kiss that was both sweet and soft, but it held a hint of passion, and it was that hint that had her body screaming at her when she moved away after their lips parted.

She bit her lower lip, scared to look up at him, because she was afraid he'd see the messages her body was sending her. When she did look up, she saw that he'd sat back, his eyes searching hers. Their eyes locked and did a lot of communicating all on their own, but neither of them moved. It was Rhiannon who broke the spell by clearing her throat.

"I better be going," she said, reaching for the door handle.

"I'll get it," he said, and got out of the car to go around to her side.

He opened the door, and when she got out she stopped. His hand went to her waist and he pulled her to him again, his kiss stronger this time. There was no mistaking the passion behind it, and Rhiannon was sure her knees were going to give out on her. It had been so long since a man had kissed her—and on top of it, Kyle Masterson could kiss! Her entire body was warmed in his embrace, in the feel of his lips. She was sure she was going crazy. When the kiss ended, he looked down into her eyes for a long moment.

"Goodnight, Rhiannon," he said softly.

Rhiannon nodded, not trusting her voice to speak. She walked over to her car and watched as he pulled his around to sit behind hers, waiting to follow her out of the parking lot. Something else Jason had always done, never leaving first, even before they were a couple. She smiled wistfully at the thought.

On the drive home, it occurred to her that for once she'd thought of Jason without feeling that deep sense of pain. Maybe she was finally healing. Maybe it was okay that she was feeling whole, even if it might be just for now.

You can find more information about the author and series here:

www.sherrylhancock.com

www.facebook.com/SherrylDHancock

www.vulpine-press.com/midknight-blue-series

Also by Sherryl D. Hancock:

The *WeHo* series follows a group of women from Los Angeles as they navigate the ups and downs of love, life, work, and everything in between.

www.vulpine-press.com/we-ho

The *Wild Irish Silence* series. Escape into the world of BJ Sparks and discover how he went from the small-town boy to the world-famous rock star.

www.vulpine-press.com/wild-irish-silence-series